Seanche's Lament

Author:

Ian McGarty

Editor:

Jeff Harkness

Layout:

Suzy Moseby

Art Director:

Casey Christofferson

Front Cover Art:

Thuan Pham

Interior Art:

C.J. Marsh, Michael Syrigos, Josh Stewart, Lloyd Metcalf, Terry Pavlet, Thuan Pham, Hector Rodriguez, Brett Barkley

Cartography:

Robert Altbauer

Project Manager:

Edwin Nagy

Swords & Wizardry Conversion:

Jeff Harkness

Frog God Games is:

Bill Webb, Matt Finch, Zach Glazar, Charles A. Wright, Edwin Nagy, Mike Badolato, and John Barnhouse

Frog God Games

Adventures Worth Winning

Frog God Games

ISBN: 978-1-6656-0149-8

SW PoD

Table of Contents

Introduction 3
The Story 3
Gnaddr 3
The Seanche 3
Regional Map 4
The Timeline 4
Some Stories and Associated Encounters 4
  The First Tale 4
  The Second Tale 5
  The Third Tale 5
  The Fourth Tale 5
The Adventure Begins 6
1. Fenlow 6
  1-B. A Court of the Fey 6
2. Traveling to the Next Village 6
3. Arklow 7
Doirche's Cave Map 8
  Doirche's Cave 8
    1. Cave Entrance 8
    2. Skinning Room 8
    3. Peat Maze 8
    4. Storage Room 9
    Challenges While Tracking 9
    The Wolfpack 10
4. A Forked Tongue in the Path 10
5. Carlow 11
  5-A. The Red Shoe 11
  5-B. Wizard's Weal Tavern 11
    The Seanche in Carlow 11
6. Wicklow 12
  6-A. Fenlaugh Fish 12
  6-B. The Smart Salmon 12
    The Seanche in Wicklow 12
The Emerald Plains 13
7. Tabla An-Mohr 13
  7-A. The Giant's Feast Cave formations 13
    1. Rock Pile 13
    2. Cave Entrance 13
    3. Cave 13
    4. The Main Dish 13
Giant's Feast Map 14
  7-B. The Queen of the Emerald Serpents 15
Queen of the Emerald Serpent's Cave Map 16
8. Bru Na Brighid 16
  8-A. Brighid's Rest 16
  8-B. Senan's Sundry Shop 16
    The Seanche in Bru Na Brighid 17

8-C. Brighid's Shrine 17
  1. Main Chamber 17
  2. Treasure Pit 17
  3. Upper Chamber 17
9. The Lazy Lake 18
  1. "Bring me the metal." 18
  2. "Help me smelt the ore." 18
  3. "Help me pour the ore." 18
  4. "Help me shatter the mold." 18
10. The Hartwood 19
The Hartwood Map 20
  10-1. Traveling in the Hartwood 20
  10-2. Eo Mughna 20
  Seanche's Lament 20
    1. The Characters Arrive First 20
    2. The Characters Arrive with the Seanche 20
    3. The Seanche Arrives Before the Characters 21
Conclusion 21
Appendix A: New Monsters 22
  Bean Fionn 22
  Each-uisce 22
  Ekimmu 22
  Elemental Adders 23
  Emerald Naga 23
  Fear Ghorta 24
  Fey Lord 24
  Fey Lupe 24
  Filth Fairy 25
  Giant Pike 25
  Phooka 25
  Summer Knight 26
  Swarm of Grigs 26
Appendix B: New Magic Items 27
  Brighid's Raiment and Arms 27
    Brighid's Breastplate 27
    Brighid's Spear 27
    Brighid's Shield 27
  Miscellaneous Magical Item, Greater 27
    Torc na Goineog 27
  Miscellaneous Magical Items, Medium 27
    Leprechaun's Gold 27
  Weapons 27
    Deadly Whisper 27
    Feyslayer Sword 27
  Cursed Item 27
    Luricawne Shoes 27
    Uillean Pipes of Reality 27

Seanche's Lament

By Ian McGarty

A Swords & Wizardry adventure designed for four to six characters of 3rd to 5th level

Introduction

The Seanche's Lament is a *Swords & Wizardry* adventure for four to six characters of 3rd to 5th level. The characters begin this adventure on the road, traveling in a civilized kingdom in an area with farming villages and a bucolic countryside. It is designed to be placed into any campaign you are playing but it has a decidedly Eurocentric feel due to the Irish and Celtic folklore that was explored to create it. The adventure itself is set up to follow a timeline of actions, but this is a sandbox adventure where characters may wander to whatever locations they wish. The adventure begins 18 days after a new moon as the characters arrive at the village of Fenlow.

The Story

The Seanche (*shana-khi*) is a legendary performer who travels the lands spreading news and joy. Stories of his musical prowess precede him. It is unclear whether Seanche is a title passed from one great performer to the next, or if the Seanche is a supernatural being who has traveled the lands for hundreds of years.

Recently, the Seanche began sharing a decidedly dark story, and the fey magic woven into these enrapturing tales is wreaking havoc in the wake of his travels. Seven years ago, the Seanche made a terrible wager, and the cursed *uilleann (you-lin) pipes of reality* (see **Appendix B: New Magic Items**) he bears were his reward. The Seanche participated in a contest of musical skill against Gnaddr (*nadd er*), a disguised fey lord. Gnaddr knew the Seanche would win as he was the most renowned performer in a large area. Built into Gnaddr's "gift" of the *uillean pipes* was a curse that began on the new moon 18 days ago and grew in power and urgency.

Lamenting his woe, the Seanche now travels into wild and untamed lands, heading for less populated areas to minimize the damage caused by his curse and his ego. Unfortunately, the Seanche's seemingly good intentions are actually an urge created by the curse to bring the Seanche to the Eo Mughna (*eye-oh muk-na*) located deep in the Hartwood. The sadness of his curse can be seen in his eyes as he is compelled to play hauntingly beautiful songs that materialize into reality and spread the chaos that Gnaddr desires. The Seanche knows his tour of terror is coming to an end.

Gnaddr, the Serpent Priest, is a fey creature clad in scintillating green scale armor whose beauty is nearly painful to behold. He spreads an aura of charisma, and the weak-minded find it easy to simply follow his suggestions. He tricked the Seanche and forced him to use the *uillean pipes of reality* to manifest enough creatures from his nearby plane to gain a physical foothold in this realm. Even now, his power grows as the chaos increases and the veil between realms thins with the approach of the full moon. With the full moon on the eve of Imbolc (*im-olg*), the Seanche arrives at the Eo Mughna and completes the ritual. Gnaddr attempts to sacrifice the Seanche's life and musical prowess to solidify the bridge to allow Gnaddr's army to cross into this realm.

> Uilleann pipes are a type of bagpipe consisting of a bellows placed under one arm, a bag, a chanter, which is often set on a piece of leather when played, three drones, and a regulator. The drones play continuously once they are switched on, while the chanter produces two octaves of notes using seven holes. Uilleann, which means elbow, refers to the bellows that is pumped to allow the bag to remain filled. A benefit of the uilleann pipes is that it allows the musician to sing while playing and it produces a rich, layered sound with a portable instrument.

Gnaddr

This fey lord fancies himself the Serpent Priest. He acquired the *torc na goineog* (see **Appendix B: New Magic Items**) from the emerald naga queen's realm and used it to force the emerald nagas to assist him. The nagas are following the exact letter of the deal they made with Gnaddr to "harass and terrify the local populace." To this end, they are simply traveling around the area in small packs and stealing tasty livestock. Strangely, the local villagers are finding valuable emeralds in the shape of scales near the sites where their livestock disappear. The populace interpreted this as a boon, although reports of giant snakes are now common.

Gnaddr's goal is to bridge the gap between this plane and his own so he can bring his army across. If his army can control this area, it weakens the veil between his plane and the Material Plane and allows his own reality to spill in and take over the area.

Gnaddr did not travel to this realm alone. Thus far, he has not managed to strengthen his hold on this realm enough to allow his army to get through. But his personal retinue and one of his lieutenants and her group of soldiers support him. He is always with his retinue of fey lupes, although they are often hidden from view. His lieutenant, Lady

Puinseann (*pun shun*), is his hands and eyes in the land and attempts to thwart the characters if possible. If she survives earlier encounters with the characters, she is at the Hartwood with Gnaddr. If the characters delay or hamper the Seanche, Gnaddr sends a pack of **12 fey lupes** to harass and hamper them. They attempt to sneak into range of the characters, attack once, and then slip away. They repeat these hit-and-run attacks until killed or driven off.

Fey Lupes (12): HD 2; **AC** 7[12]; **Atk** 2 claws (1d4); **Move** 12 or pounce (30ft leap); **Save** 16; **AL** C; **CL/XP** 3/60; **Special:** darkvision (60ft), howl (1/day, each pack member gains 1 hp per fey lupe joining in), immune to charm and sleep, pounce (30ft leap), rend (if 2 claws hit target, additional 1d4 damage, save avoids).

The Seanche

The Seanche is a human man in his late 30s or early 40s. He has a well-trimmed red beard that matches his light red hair. He always carries his *uilleann pipes of reality*, which are crafted from the most exquisite honey-brown wood and fitted with gold settings, and a bag crafted from the velvet-soft hide of a white stag. His clothes are finely crafted but show the wear and stain of a life spent continuously on the road.

This cursed performer's mournful songs are often the only glimpse of him the characters obtain if they encounter him outside a tavern or stage. Over the course of his travels, the Seanche picked up some unique spellcasting talents.

The Seanche, Male Human Cursed Performer: HP 74; **AC** 7[12]; **Atk** +1 longsword (1d8+1); **Move** 12; **Save** 5; **AL** L; **CL/XP** 12/2000; **Special:** spells (cast as a 10th-level spellcaster).

Spells: 3/day—*charm person, cure light wounds, darkness 15ft radius, detect invisibility, invisibility, light, magic missile, obscuring mist, phantasmal force*; 2/day—*dispel magic, haste*; 1/day—*confusion, fear, hallucinatory terrain*; 1/week—*legend lore*.

Equipment: +1 longsword, leather armor, *uilleann pipes of reality* (see **Appendix B: New Magic Items**).

Note: The Seanche is cursed by the uilleann pipes he carries. They force him to perform a song each night and are leading him toward the Hartwood.

> ### Playing the Seanche
>
> This cursed performer's goal is always to escape any sort of combat. He uses spells to hide and then quickly slips away. He relies upon the *uilleann pipes of destiny* in order to aid his escape and avoids direct physical combat. The Seanche relies upon spells to evade and disorient his enemies. He is loath to permanently harm his opponents and uses illusions to trap his enemies while he escapes. One of his favorite ploys is to first cast an illusory double directly on top of himself using *phantasmal force*. He then uses *invisibility* on his next turn to run away while his double heads in the other direction. Be clever with his actions and remember that above all, his goal is to escape.
>
> The Seanche uses the pipe's magical spells such as *dimension door* and *transport via plants* to aid his escape. In a pinch, the pipes themselves protect the Seanche and aid his escape. If cornered, the pipes emit a heavy, dull note. All creatures within 60 feet other than the Seanche who hear the note must make a saving throw with a −4 penalty or be petrified for 12 hours.

The Seanche's goal is to get to the Hartwood; the pipes are drawing him there and causing him to manifest a song each night. The characters encounter the effects of the Seanche's presence for two days before they first encounter the Seanche. Barring plot-bending efforts by the characters, it takes nine more days for the Seanche to reach the Hartwood.

As the Seanche travels, he is beholden to the curse of the *uilleann pipes of reality*. The curse has these key components:

1. The Seanche may not spend more than one night in any settlement.
2. He must perform to an audience each night.
3. When traveling, he is under the effects of a *transport via plants* spell.

THE TIMELINE

The cursed Seanche overnights in Fenlow then travels for two days before the characters encounter him in Arklow. During this time, they hear rumors of his travels and see the effects of the curse. They first encounter the Seanche outside Arklow on Night 2 and see the direct manifestation of the curse the next day.

THE SEANCHE'S TRAVELS

Night	Seanche's Location	Characters' Possible Locations
1	Bandit camp outside Fenlow	Fenlow
2	A farm outside Arklow	Arklow, where they encounter the Seanche and hear *The Tale of the Magician and the Deer*
3	On the road	Chat with Fhirin and decide a course
4	Carlow	If the characters are here, they hear *The Tale of Luricawne and the Cobbler*
5	Wicklow	If the characters are here, they hear *The Tale of the Giant Pike*
6	On the road*	
7	Bru Na Brighid	If the characters are here, they hear *The Tale of the Farmer and the Leprechaun*
8	On the road*	
9	On the road*	
10	The Hartwood	Characters should catch up to the Seanche here within a few days.

* If the party is with the Seanche any of these nights, feel free to choose one of the four tales below or create your own.

If the characters catch up to him, they may travel with him for a day but each night he sings a song and triggers an encounter. These encounters always occur after the Seanche performs. Describe the tale he sings, then place the encounter in the most appropriate spot through the night and next day. Like any savvy wanderer, the Seanche attempts to trade song for a spot in a barn or around a campfire. If combat occurs, he slips away, if possible.

SOME STORIES AND ASSOCIATED ENCOUNTERS

As the characters travel, they may find themselves in the company of the Seanche. If so, he always ends the night with a song. The following four tales can be used as the characters camp.

THE FIRST TALE

The Seanche begins a woeful tale of a poor man who starved to death during a famine. He wandered the countryside, begging for the help of others, but he fell by the side of the road and died. His undiscovered and unshriven body was consumed by the land. This spirit, still hungry for food and life, now haunts unwary travelers. This creature appears to be a gaunt, emaciated figure clad in tattered clothes. Rags are wrapped around his feet, and he shuffles unsteadily with each step. He clutches a crudely carved and worn wooden bowl. If he is not offered food, he mumbles quietly to himself and shuffles off into the darkness.

Throughout the night, the group's sleep is disturbed by moaning and the shrieks of a **fear ghorta**. A creature who hears the creature must succeed on a saving throw or be unable to rest (and suffer a –1 penalty to hit, damage, and saves next day). The old man shuffles toward the characters' camp and humbly extends his bowl. If he is refused, his tattered robes begin fluttering although there is no wind. Faster and faster, they whip around him until they come to rest and reveal a gaunt, long-limbed creature with leathery skin stretched taut across an impossibly long face with a gaping toothless opening of pure blackness serving as a mouth. If destroyed, it whispers in a hoarse voice, *"Even through the ground, I hunger ..."*

When the fear ghorta's gaunt form materializes, a patch of strangely lush green grass also grows within 60 feet of the characters' campsite. The hungry grass begins draining 1d6 hit points per hour from all characters within range. If the grass is destroyed, the characters discover a crudely buried body haphazardly tossed in a hasty grave. Holy water, a proper burial in a marked grave, or a cleric's blessing can consecrate the grave and allow the fear ghorta to finally feel sated and achieve the rest it desperately desires. If the characters do not discover and consecrate the body, the grass regrows each night (roll 1d6 to determine how many hours after midnight it happens). The fear ghorta's gaunt form rematerializes each night at that time to torment the group. Until the body is consecrated or destroyed, the fear ghorta and the hungry grass reappear each night.

Fear Ghorta: HD 8; HP 57; AC 6[13]; Atk withering touch (1d6); **Move** 12; Save 8; AL C; CL/XP 10/1400; **Special:** famish (3/day, 30ft radius, save or take 1d6 damage for 1d4 rounds and eat any available food), hungry grass (60ft radius, drain life, 1d6 damage per hour), howl (save or unable to sleep, –1 penalty to hit, damage, and saves until able to rest), vulnerable to fire (200% damage). (see **Appendix A: New Monsters**)

The Second Tale

The Seanche sings a tale describing a handsome young man with a voice as sweet as wildflower honey. This man's arrogance and pride swell, until they and that sweet voice are all that are left of him. But these vices are his undoing, for he encounters a fey lord clad in shining green armor who claims his voice is more beautiful than the young man's. The green fey lord offers a set of uilleann pipes crafted from the most exquisite wood with gold settings and a bag crafted from the hide of a white stag.

The young man wins the contest and receives the pipes. But these beautiful pipes curse the young man to travel the land and sing the tales of curses and creatures, which allow them to materialize to terrorize people and cause chaos. He sings of a journey that ends in a dark forest at a magnificent yew with bark of silver and gold. There, the Serpent Priest forces him to sing a bridge into reality to allow a monstrous army to invade the lands. The cost of the bridge is the young man's life, and the Seanche sings of his empty husk drained of its power and life. Not even the most intrepid could stop him.

At this point, he stands and asks a question: "What will you do?" As he waits, the uilleann pipes continue their steady drone.

Obviously, the characters may notice the similarities between the instrument the Seanche is describing and the instrument he happens to be playing. The tree in the song is the Eo Mughna, a mighty yew in the Hartwood, a local forest.

When the Seanche asks the characters what they will do, he activated the song and left a magical duplicate of himself to deal with the characters. If they are aggressive, have them roll initiative and begin the battle with a **shadow Seanche**, an exact duplicate of the Seanche that fights without mercy to halt the characters. While nearly an exact duplicate of the real Seanche, the shadow Seanche's false pipes create a thunderous wave that does 1d8 points of damage to all creatures within 30 feet and forces them to make a saving throw or be deafened for 12 hours.

Shadow Seanche: HP 74; AC 7[12]; **Atk** *+1 longsword* (1d8+1); **Move** 12; Save 5; AL L; CL/XP 12/2000; **Special:** spells (cast as a 10th-level spellcaster).
Spells: 3/day—*charm person, cure light wounds, darkness 15ft radius, detect invisibility, invisibility, light, magic missile, obscuring mist, phantasmal force;* 2/day—*dispel magic, haste;* 1/day—*confusion, fear, hallucinatory terrain;* 1/week—*legend lore.*
Equipment: *+1 longsword*, leather armor, false *uilleann pipes of reality.*
Note: The shadow Seanche's equipment evaporates if it is killed.

The Third Tale

The Seanche sings a tale of three fey sisters who lived in the forest near a village. They had lived in those woods for longer than men had been near. But as the village grew, the forest was cleared by the villagers and consumed by a growing urban settlement. The fey sisters were corrupted and turned into twisted perversions of what they once were.

The next day, **3 filth fairies** ambush the characters.
Filth Fairies (3): HD 4; HP 31, 29, 24; AC 5[14]; **Atk** 2 claws (1d4 + 1d3 acid); **Move** 12 (fly 12, swim 12); **Save** 13; AL C; CL/XP 5/240; **Special:** acidic (additional 1d3 damage), slime breath (3/day, 15ft cone, 3d6 acid damage, save for half), spell-like abilities. (see **Appendix A: New Monsters**)
Spell-like abilities: at will—*faerie fire, obscuring mist;* 3/day—*phantasmal force.*

The Fourth Tale

On this dark and cool night with a view of the nearly full moon, the Seanche joins you at the fire once again. With an apologetic look and a sigh, he brings out the beautiful uilleann pipes and begins a song. This strange song has a discordant melody that echoes into the night as the Seanche begins a song of the Moon being lonely each night and longing for someone to spend time within the darkness. She enacts a plan that severs the shadows from Brighid's followers. The shadows dance with her each night but when Brighid finds out, she flies to the Moon's palace on a horse of fire and demands the shadows back. The Moon acquiesces and returns the shadows, but her immense sadness touches Brighid's heart. She tells the Moon that she will force the Sun to stay alight while the Moon visits as often as possible. This is why we sometimes see the Moon in the mornings or afternoons.

"Behind you," the Seanche whispers as tears fall from his eyes.

The shadows of the characters are severed from their bodies and immediately attack. A **severed shadow** of each character now exists. When the battle begins, the Seanche slips off into the night, if possible.

Severed Shadows

Severed shadows are shadowy duplicates of the characters. They appear with the same weapons and armor, all composed of a shadowy substance. These duplicates have the same hit points, armor class, and abilities as the characters. However, these malicious shadows exist only to destroy their material counterparts so they can remain in their stead.

In addition to the characters' abilities, the severed shadows have a 50% chance of vanishing while in dim light or darkness.

If a character is killed by its shadow self, the shadow merges with the corpse and rises as a living — and evil — version of the character. Nothing short of a *wish* can restore the original character.

The Adventure Begins

The adventure begins on the road as the characters travel toward another destination. The roads in this area are wide dirt paths with occasional stretches of cobblestone or gravel in the wettest areas. It is clear someone regularly maintains the road. The locals are preparing to celebrate Imbolc, a festival to welcome spring. This festival also honors the local deity Brighid, who is a goddess of poets, smiths, and healers. She often appears clad in bronze armor and wreathed in flames or sunlight. The local people are excited this year due to the early thaw; crops are already sprouting in the fields.

1. Fenlow

The first signs of an approaching village materialize on the horizon. Farmers and workers are in the fields, and animals graze in pens or are tended by shepherds. The people are friendly, and children and adults alike offer a friendly wave. The village proper is small and quaint. A general store, a tavern with generous outdoor seating, a stable and blacksmith, and a 30-foot-tall stone tower sit alongside the well-worn dirt road. Chickens, dogs, and cats wander the town looking for refuse.

Standing outside the tower are a young man in chainmail holding a spear and an older, thickly bearded man with clothes made of fine materials worn with age and use, vestiges of a wealth that seems to have faded. The young man is talking animatedly, gesturing with his free hand and pointing toward the forest.

The guards are discussing a missing boy. The characters can learn that he's been kidnapped, but he's also at home as a fey creature replaced the local boy with a changeling. The party learns that the young guard discovered an area in the forest where the fey are entering and saw the missing boy and a fey lord with his retinue.

Young Guard, Male Human (Rgr2): HP 18; AC 7[12]; **Atk** longsword (1d8) or longbow x2 (1d6); **Move** 12; **Save** 13; **AL** L; **CL/XP** 2/30; **Special:** +2 damage vs. giants and goblin-types, alertness, tracking. **Equipment:** leather armor, longsword, longbow, 20 arrows.

Speaking with anyone in the village reveals the following to the characters:

1. A famous performer known as the Seanche passed through the village yesterday afternoon. He shared news of the kingdom, local area gossip, and sang songs and shared a story.
2. Last night, the Seanche shared a story about a farmer's son who was kidnapped by the fey and replaced with a changeling. The local kids are playing out the story in the streets.
3. A village less than a week away captured a leprechaun and acquired his gold. But now mysterious tragedies are occurring in the town.
4. The Seanche shared a story of a cursed poet who angered a dryad and was forced to watch as the tales he sang became real. In the story, the poet dies alone, hiding in a cave for fear of harming someone.
5. The predicted light snows and mild winter led to early crops and excitement in the area. It is a good year for the villages in the area.
6. Giant snake swarms have been seen in the area but they haven't harmed anyone yet.
7. Tommy Riordan found three huge flat emeralds in his cattle pen after three goats went missing. He thinks brownies left him a gift after taking the animals.

1-B. A Court of the Fey

The young guardsman immediately offers to accompany the characters to the area in the forest where he saw the fey lord holding court. It was in the deep forest, and the guardsman explains that even the most experienced woodsfolk lose their way reaching the area and getting back. It takes three hours to reach the fey lord's impromptu court, but add 1d3 additional hours if the characters don't accept the guard's offer to show them the path. Read the following, adjusting as needed if the guard is not with the characters:

The forest is a tangle of undergrowth and tree limbs as you struggle to keep pace with the young guard. He pauses every few moments to allow the slower members of the group the opportunity to catch up but he coaxes them along each time. Without warning, the thick forest breaks open into a clearing roughly 50 feet across. A small stream gurgles its way across an edge of this clearing, and a handsome elf with aquiline features holds his nose haughtily in the air as he watches your group stumble into the clearing. Several figures in intricate armor crafted of some sort of metallic leaves stand around the edges of the clearing, and a woven basket sits beside the fey lord's ornate and beautifully carved wooden throne. A small baby coos and gurgles happily in its wicker bassinet as it nestles amid lush green leaves sprouting from still-living branches.

The **fey lord** kidnapped this child but may be convinced to release the boy. He does so in exchange for any of the following: a replacement child, a magical item, or one year of a character's life.

"Aaah, visitors! Welcome to my impromptu spring court. I assume you have come to show obeisance at my feet? The village has already gifted me this beautiful child. It will be a strong addition to the servants of my court. Perhaps you are also here to pledge your fealty and join my retinue?" The fey lord speaks in a haughty and demeaning manner.

The fey lord is manipulative in his negotiations and attempts to use language to sweeten the deal in his favor. The characters may also attempt to put a loophole into whatever options they present and should be rewarded for creativity and cleverness (e.g., the chaste cleric offers her firstborn child).

If the encounter turns to combat, the fey lord is in his lair and protected by a retinue of **8 elf warriors**.

If the characters are able to return the child, the town rewards them 50 gp and the lord gifts them a family heirloom. This may be any *+1 weapon* you determine.

Fey Lord: HD 7; HP 49; AC 2[17]; **Atk** rapier (1d6) or slap (1d4); **Move** 12; **Save** 9; **AL** N; **CL/XP** 8/800; **Special:** +1 or better magic weapons to hit, immune to charm and sleep, magic resistance (15%), spell-like abilities, vulnerable to iron (200% damage). **Spell-like abilities:** at will—*charm person, faerie fire, light, sleep*; 3/day—*clairvoyance, dimension door, ESP, invisibility, plant growth, polymorph self*; 1/day—*ice storm*.

Elf Warriors (8): HD 3; AC 5[14]; **Atk** longsword (1d8) or longbow x2 (1d6); **Move** 12; **Save** 14; **AL** N; **CL/XP** 3/60; **Special:** darkvision (60ft), detect secret doors (4-in-6 chance), immune to ghoul paralysis.

2. Traveling to the Next Village

Travel in this idyllic countryside is occasionally interrupted by wild or dangerous animals and even the occasional group of bandits. Read the following to the party as the day turns to night and they seek out a camp:

Ahead, a dented and scratched cart has been pulled to the side of the road and a small fire blazes nearby. Half a dozen humanoids in worn clothes and armed with a hodgepodge of secondhand weapons and scraps of armor mill around the flames. They appear to be arguing.

The bandits spot any characters who don't hide their approach. Details of the argument can be heard if the characters get close enough. The information that can be gleaned is as follows:

- The bean fíonn (*be-on-fin*), the White Lady, took Albrecht below the nearby lake to drown tonight when the moon shines brightest.
- The men are arguing about whether to rescue Albrecht or if they could give the bean fíonn something else to appease her.
- The bandits spent yesterday evening with a traveling performer who sang to them of the failure of the Lazy One, a fey creature who was off with her human lover rather than guarding a local spring. This caused extensive flooding across the countryside. The fey creature blamed the people of the land for causing this and is said to have drowned her love in order to take him into the Tuatha De Danann (*to-ah day dun-on*) to live with her forever.
- Albrecht is the only one who knows where the bandit treasure is hidden. The remaining bandits are about to draw lots to determine who's going to replace Albrecht and who's going to parley with the bean fíonn.

The bean fíonn is a beautiful humanoid who lives in the water of the nearby pond. A small island camouflaged in trees and plant growth sits in the center of this pond, and an aged wooden skiff is pulled onto the rocky beach and tied to a large boulder nearby. A character who rolls below his or her wisdom on 3d6 notices that the water appears to be rising. The boat is floating, no longer perched on the shore where it was left. At first it almost appears as though there is a tide, but no obvious inlets exist to create a current. If the pond is observed for a short time, it becomes quite clear that the water is rising, and quickly.

Anyone disturbing the water or wildlife near the pond summons the **bean fíonn**, who arrives with a bubbling of water. The bean fíonn forms from the water itself, a whirling tower of water that coalesces into a beautiful humanoid woman with pronounced elven features and exceptionally long ears. Her skin remains so pale that it is nearly blue. She speaks in a melodious voice that sparkles like soft chimes with any who approach, offering them fabulous wealth in exchange for a year in her service. In order to free the mortal she captured, she needs to be bested in some contest.

The bean fíonn is smart, coldhearted, and prone to tricking characters. She offers the characters a straight exchange of one mortal soul for another but accepts a reasonable challenge provided by the characters. This takes some ingenuity and creativity on your part. The bean fíonn cheats if she is able to do so. However, if she feels cheated or dislikes the results, she may simply attack. If she is attacked, she immediately emits a high-pitched whistle that summons her pack of **6 phookas**. They understand that this means she is under attack and attempt to surprise her opponents by using their tree stride ability to surprise and ambush the characters. If the bean fíonn is defeated, her lair may be discovered by diving below the water. Her lair is beyond a cave entrance that opens into a small grotto lush with plants, small cascading pools, and beds of strand strewn with random personal items. Items are tucked into the stone walls or sit on shelves where there are no plants. Most of these items are mundane items from the mortal realm that she has collected. But tucked among this hodgepodge of items are *gauntlets of swimming and climbing*, a *jug of alchemy*, and a *bag of holding* containing seven assorted gems worth 35 gp each. The bean fíonn's captured human is also lying on a sandbar, glassy eyed and confused. This charm wears off once he is free of the bean fíonn's lair.

Bean Fíonn: HD 7; **HP** 50; **AC** 7[12]; **Atk** claws (1d4); **Move** 12 (swim 12); **Save** 9; **AL** N; **CL/XP** 8/800; **Special:** beguiling kiss (3/day, save or charmed for 1 hour), drowning tide (1/day, 15ft radius, 2d6 cold damage, save for half), immune to charm and sleep, resist cold (50% damage). (see **Appendix A: New Monsters**)

Phookas (6): HD 4; **HP** 30, 27, 26, 22x2, 17; **AC** 5[14]; **Atk** dagger (1d3); **Move** 6; **Save** 13; **AL** N; **CL/XP** 5/240; **Special:** alternate form (at will, mountain lion or wolf), dancing lights (3/day, moving balls of light), spell resistance (16%), tree stride (enter tree and move up to 50ft to another tree). (see **Appendix A: New Monsters**)

Interacting with the Fey

The fey are selfish and capricious, always seeking favor and advantage. Due to their long lives, they are willing to play a long game in order to get what they want. Ideally, they draw anyone they deal with into their stories and goals, making them characters in the play and story tropes that they must re-enact. They may be found acting out older legends and stories with new victims. Their glamour and charisma is palpable and infectious, which is why many common folk find themselves pulled into a fey creature's plans before they realize they had a chance to escape. They are fickle and can be emotionally unpredictable, shifting from carefree and laughing to anger and violence in the blink of an eye. But they also crave interaction and the adoration of humans and demihumans, and they seem to somehow gain strength from these interactions. If the characters "win" an encounter with a fey creature, it may be because they are fulfilling a trope or a need for the story that the fey is attempting to recreate.

3. Arklow

This small cluster of stone and wooden buildings is nestled amid rolling hills and verdant farmland. Children run between buildings and play in the open spaces. Arklow consists of a roadside public house, a grain mill alongside a river that cuts through town, a general store, and several homes. Worked fields and farmhouses surround the village itself. Animals idly meander through the green fields.

A great deal of noise comes from the public house, where you hear the joyful buzz of people gathering, laughing, talking, and playing music.

The public house is packed with people and moving through this dense crowd of people is difficult.

The characters enter just as a man (the Seanche) in a rich brown doublet that has seen years of wear despite being well cared for takes the stage. His face appears jovial, with a wide smile, but his eyes are deep emerald pools that are worn with sorrow. He has a well-trimmed red beard that matches his light red hair. He holds his uillean pipes in his lap. He begins tuning the instrument, pumping the bag with his arm and elbow, and the crowd hushes themselves. Allow the characters time to get a drink and table and to carouse awhile.

The man begins singing a sweet and mournful ballad that immediately silences the crowd. His voice and the instrument combine to create a harmonious coupling that nears perfection.

Roll 1d6 on the table below and add +1 for each character who succeeds on a saving throw:

1d6	Effect Noticed
1–4	There is something magical about this tune.
5–7	The effect is not influencing people but it is drawing something from them.
8+	The effect of the magic emanating from the lute and this man's voice is drawing some power or lifeforce in small portions from everyone in the crowd.

The music doesn't cause any lasting damage but anyone who failed the previous saving throw feels exhausted the next day (–1 to hit and damage).

The song describes a young person who lost his wife when an evil magician turned her into a deer for seven years. When he finally caught the magician, he found that the mage had killed and eaten his wife, but the child she was carrying escaped as a deer.

The Seanche moves to a table and begins sharing news of neighboring villages and the kingdom. The characters may speak to him, and this is an excellent spot to insert future adventure hooks, news of your campaign world, and general rumors. You can also use the generic rumor table below:

1d8	Rumor
1	A terrifying leviathan has been harassing fishing vessels along the coast and destroying nets and traps.
2	A farmer in a nearby village is said to have created a truly delightful whiskey this year.
3	The tax collector was spotted a few weeks away, right on schedule.
4	It is nearly mating season for the local deer, and it looks to be a healthy herd this year.
5	Fungus infected the crops of several nearby farmers, and they may be looking for spare seed on loan or for coin if they must.
6	Sam Hasting had a cow go missing last week but he found a huge strangely cut and valuable emerald in the pen. A fey must have taken the cow and left him the gift.
7	The child of a wealthy nearby landowner is coming of age in several months and they are hearing out potential suitors.
8	Wolves have been chasing people in the Hartwood.

The crowd clears well before midnight, and the people leave tired but happy. The Seanche disappears with the crowd to a room provided by the house. He leaves in the morning before the characters notice. They may spot him if extreme measures and some creativity are supplied by the characters. If so, he can be seen disappearing into the darkness. The faint melody of a vaguely familiar tune can be heard carried on the breeze as he departs.

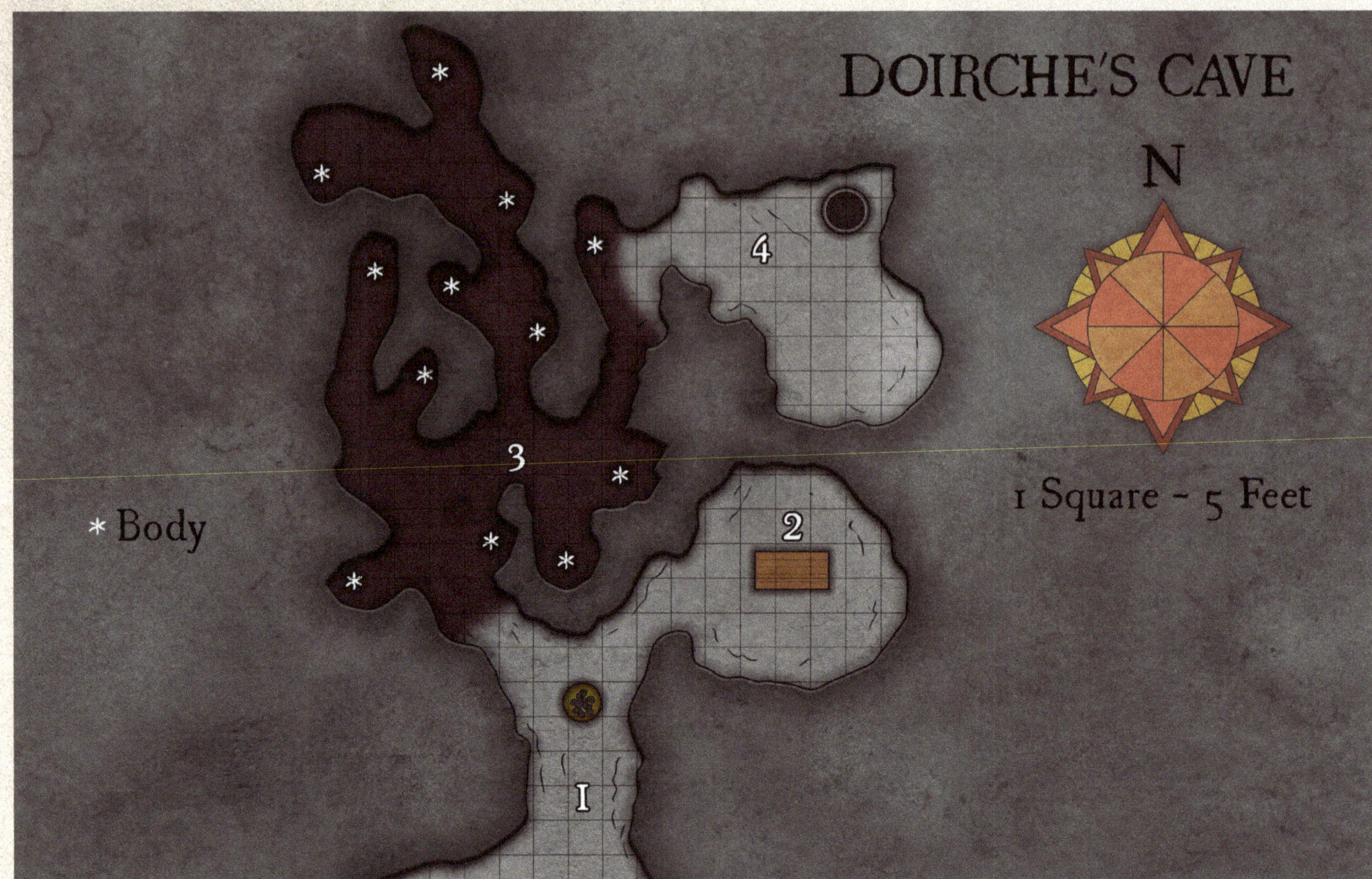

If the characters continue their journey on the road, they happen across a large farm with outbuildings and smaller houses placed among the fields. The main farmstead contains several buildings within a five-foot-high stone wall made from gathered fieldstones. A commotion is occurring in front of the buildings with men and women shouting and arming themselves with convenient field tools and a few older swords or spears. As the characters approach, people can be overheard talking about hunting and killing the doirche (*door-ka*) who cast the curse.

> "We know where he is, I say we burn him out!"
>
> "Yeah! … We can't let this stand."
>
> "He could come back and turn any of us!"
>
> "Let's go!"

This fearful mob of angry villagers is armed with a variety of farming implements, several rusty swords, and axes. They appear to be genuine in those feelings and without apparent duplicitousness. Speaking with the group reveals that a magician turned the young farmer's wife into a deer yesterday evening. They tracked the magician to a cave in the nearby bog only an hour or two away.

If the characters rescue the wife before the magician kills her, they can lift the curse. If they do so, the farmers reward them with an heirloom from the family (a *+1 ring of protection*) as well as 500 gp worth of assorted coins. The group sends Rory Shalgur, an adept hunter and tracker who is familiar with the area, to guide the characters. They explain that this stretch of woods can be difficult to navigate, especially lately with things seeming to shift occasionally. If the characters wish to go alone, Rory provides directions and the players have a 35% chance (+15% for every elf or ranger in the party). If they are successful, they locate the doirche's cave. If they fail, they end up back at the edge of the forest where the villagers are waiting.

Rory Shalgur, Male Human (Rgr5): HP 37; **AC** 7[12]; **Atk** *+1 short sword* (1d6+1) or longbow x2 (1d6); **Move** 12; **Save** 10; **AL** L; **CL/ XP** 5/240; **Special:** +5 damage vs. giants and goblin-types, alertness, tracking.
Equipment: leather armor, short sword, longbow, 20 arrows.

Doirche's Cave

As the characters approach the cave, they spot bone totems placed around the area and hung with chimes made from larger leg and arm bones. The bones belonged to various animals, goblins, and orcs. The guide remains just beyond the first totem as he points out the cave ahead, which seems to sprout from the bog and provides an island that drops into the peat around it.

1. Cave Entrance

This small rock- and peat-walled cave seems to absorb noise. An iron brazier hanging from the ceiling sputters and hisses as it casts dim light through this room. Crude glyphs and pictographs are carved into the walls, and two exits veer off in nearly opposite directions.

2. Skinning Room

The coppery scent of aged blood tweaks your nose and tingles on your tongue as you enter this room. A crude wooden table with a variety of skinning and butcher knives rest in a pottery bowl. The tabletop is dark with bloodstains and marred with numerous cuts and gouges. Several hides are stretched across the walls and held in place with wooden pegs. There are no other exits from this room.

3. Peat Maze

This maze-like series of tunnels is studded with long dead, desiccated bodies buried in the peat. Their leathery skin and clothes are preserved but bear a ruddy hue that matches the red hair upon their heads. The red coloration is due to an extended stay in a grave of peat. A total of 13 desiccated and withered bodies, both men and women, are in the room. You can determine their races to best match your campaign and setting. These bodies are all cursed by the doirche, and each has a silver amulet beneath their clothes that is slightly sunken into their skin. This pendant is etched with intricate runes and is the source of their curse. While the characters examine the bodies, **13 shadows** attack. Casting *dispel magic*, *dispel evil*, or *remove curse* on a body and amulet destroys a corresponding shadow and releases the body's trapped soul. Casting any spell that creates light directly at the bodies stuns the shadow for the duration of the spell. If the shadows are destroyed, they rematerialize in 1d4 x 10 minutes unless the bodies are destroyed, too. If the bodies are destroyed, the amulets lose their magical aura but may be recovered and are worth 19 gp each.

Shadows (13): HD 2+2; **HP** 17, 15x2, 14, 13x2, 12x3, 10, 7, 6x2; **AC** 7[12]; **Atk** touch (1d4 + strength drain); **Move** 12; **Save** 16; **AL** C; **CL/XP** 4/120; **Special:** +1 or better magic weapons to hit, strength drain (1 point with hit, death at 0 strength). (*Monstrosities* 418)

4. STORAGE ROOM

This large cave is brimming with small shelves, gourds, and jars hanging from twine in the ceiling. The ceiling is only eight feet high at its tallest and irregularly shaped. This limits the use of large two-handed weapons (−2 penalty to attacks and damage). A large iron cauldron rests on stones, and hot coals smolder beneath it. The air is hazy with smoke and reduces visibility. The smoke is thick and pungent with the smell of burnt peat. The **doirche** stands ready to engage the party with a spell when he first sees the group. If the group simply destroys the doirche, it will be difficult for them to find the proper incantation to return the cursed farmer's wife to her true form. The incantation is scrawled on a veiny vellum sheet in a spidery script. If the doirche is subdued, he exchanges his life for the information the party seeks. Alternatively, if the party attempts to use diplomacy and parleys with the doirche from the start, he lifts the curse if the characters bring him the cursed woman who is currently in the form of a deer. However, he requires a gift worth 50 gp in exchange for his services.

Doirche, Male Mage (MU9): **HP** 31; **AC** 7[12] or 2[17] (missile) and 4[15] (melee) from *shield* spell; **Atk** *staff of power* (2d6); **Move** 12; **Save** 5 (+2, ring); **AL** N; **CL/XP** 10/1400; **Special:** +2 save (spells, wands, staffs), spells (4/3/3/2/1).
Spells: 1st—*charm person, magic missile, read magic, shield*; 2nd—*invisibility, phantasmal force, strength*; 3rd—*darkvision, fly, slow*; 4th—*confusion, polymorph other*; 5th—*hold monster*.
Equipment: *staff of power, ring of protection +2.*

Tracking the deer is a difficult task, but the guard Rory Shalgur who remained waiting can help. He knows the land and can help the characters track the deer. As the characters follow the deer, the tracks of large wolves begin appearing in the area. Rustling in the trees can be heard as the wolfpack begins its hunt. Some directionality is suggested in the writing of these challenges, but that is only to create a sense of chase with the characters; it does not matter which way the characters go as they continue to experience challenges.

CHALLENGES WHILE TRACKING

1. THE STREAM

Characters have a 45% chance to spot the trail (with a +10% chance for each elf, druid, or ranger in the party). This check is automatic if Rory Shalgur is with the party. If the trail cannot be found, the characters press on in the direction they believe the deer went. If they are reticent to pick a direction, allow a character to notice movement in a particular direction to encourage them to keep moving.

2. THE BUZZING STUMP

Anyone nearing the edge of this small clearing can discern a faint buzzing.

Roll a 1d6 each round; on a 1, the wasps see the characters. If they do, **1d3 swarms of wasps** exit the nest and make a beeline toward the characters. Continue rolling 1d6 each round combat occurs, with an additional 1d2 swarms of wasps flying out each time the characters are noticed. A total of 8 swarms can emerge before no more are left in the stump.

Swarms of Wasps (1d4 or as needed, total of 8): HD 3; AC 7[12]; **Atk** swarm (1d6); **Move** 9 (fly); **Save** 14; **AL** N; **CL/XP** 4/120; **Special:** immune to blunt weapons.

3. SALTY GRIGS

The characters have stomped into a party of doll-sized creatures and incur the wrath and ire of a **swarm of grigs**. The swarm does not pursue the characters if they attempt to escape. If the swarm engages in combat, an additional swarm of grigs arrives every three rounds and joins the fracas, until a total of three swarms engage with the characters.

Swarm of Grigs (up to 3): HD 7; AC 6[13]; **Atk** swarm (2d6); **Move** 6 (fly 9); **Save** 9; **AL** N; **CL/XP** 8/800; **Special:** fiddle, spell-like abilities. (see **Appendix A: New Monsters**)

4. THICK HEDGES

A character needs to roll below his or her dexterity on 4d6 to slip through the thorns unscathed. A failure results in 2d4 points of damage. Any creative ideas to avoid or deal with the thorns should be rewarded. Magic may also be an acceptable solution.

5. MUD PIT

Characters have a 1-in-6 chance to notice this area of soft mud obscured by leaves (3-in-6 chance for rangers, elves, and druids). If the characters cross, they immediately sink waist deep into soft mud and end up stuck. They are restrained. A character can make an Open Doors check to escape on their own or they can be pulled free by another creature. A creature trapped in the mud takes 1d6 points of damage each round.

6. THE DROP

Each character must immediately make a successful saving throw or they suffer 1d6 points of damage as they crash into trees, through saplings, and off rocks as they suddenly plummet down the hill. Each falling character must make two saving throws before they reach the bottom. Each failed saving throw causes 1d6 points of damage. They may attempt to use spells to assist them if they can cast them while tumbling down the hill.

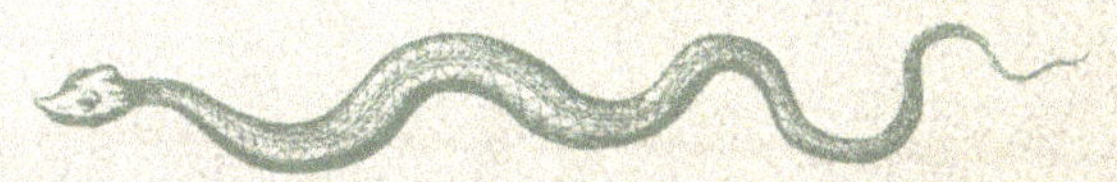

The characters finally catch up to the elusive deer, where they encounter **6 fey lupes**. The characters arrive just as the wolves begin circling the deer. These creatures are atypical and not wolves that traditionally roam the area. These wolves are larger, with dark fur that bristles along their spines. Their slavering jaws are filled with rows of sharp teeth that drip in anticipation of a meal. Their yellow eyes seem to contain a spark of intelligence. Tactically, they focus on knocking a single creature to the ground and press their advantage with as many pack members as possible. The wolves attack the deer if no other targets are near, but they turn on the party as soon as they arrive. If the deer survives, it placidly follows the characters back to the doirche to be cured or it allows a spellcaster to complete the ritual to restore it. Upon dispelling the curse, the doirche vanishes in a shower of golden sparks, leaving the wife of the farmer in her original form.

Fey Lupes (6): HD 2; HP 15, 13x2, 11, 10, 8; AC 7[12]; **Atk** 2 claws (1d4); **Move** 12 or pounce (30ft leap); **Save** 16; **AL** C; **CL/XP** 3/60; **Special:** darkvision (60ft), howl (1/day, each pack member gains 1 hp per fey lupe joining in), immune to charm and sleep, pounce (30ft leap), rend (if 2 claws hit target, additional 1d4 damage, save avoids). (see **Appendix A: New Monsters**)

4. A Forked Tongue in the Path

After leaving the second village and dealing with the doirche, you find yourselves leaving the hilly grassland as the dirt road leads into a thick, shadowy forest populated with ancient gnarled and twisted trees. After entering the first shadows of cool shade, a small clearing appears, and the path forks off in two directions. A large willow tree shades the clearing as its long limbs drape a curtain of greenery across the area.

Characters have a 2-in-6 chance to spot an emerald naga concealed in the willow. As the characters enter the clearing, the sibilant voice of **Fhirin** (*fi reen*) **the emerald naga** cautions them, "A sssssplit in your pathhhhh, perhapsssss." Fhirin then lowers herself from the tree and coils herself at the edge of the clearing.

"That way issss danger, cursessssss, and dark fey magic," Fhirin gestures to the path on the left with her tail. "Or you can choossssssse liffffffffe and ffffffffreedom." She gestures to the path on her right. "I leave it up to you." Fhirin is prepared for aggressive characters. Her goal, if the characters fight, is to poison as many characters as possible and then escape into the thick forest. Her instructions and the *geas* that compel her are to slow anyone who follows the same path as the Seanche. Fhirin only follows the letter of the *geas* she is under, as she does not like being compelled to do anything. Gnaddr has been dominating serpentkind across the countryside for several months, building toward something Fhirin does not want to hang around for.

Fhirin speaks with the characters and answers questions, although she is evasive. She may reveal the following:

- * Gnaddr knows the language of serpents and the whispers of their secrets. He wears the *torc na goineog* (*tork na go-nee-yolk*), which grants him primacy over all serpentkind and is the item that binds the emerald naga queen here.
- *The emerald naga queen is angry that Gnaddr is driving them to war with the people of the region. She has the ear of Brighid, who may grant a boon to those she favors.
- * Imbolc is fast approaching and will be a time of weal and woe.
- * She repeats this Imbolc prayer:

The serpent will come from the hole
On the brown Day of Bríde,
Though there should be three feet of snow
On the flat surface of the ground

—*Gaelic Proverb*

- * The Emerald Naga Queen SS'Thissk can be found at the Giant's Table. She loves ebony jewelry and gems.

If the characters continue on the left path following the Seanche, the road takes them to Carlow.

If the characters choose the path to the right, they soon emerge from the forest into the Emerald Plains with Tabla An-Mohr being the most obvious place in front of them.

Fhirin, Emerald Naga (Adult): HD 8; HP 55; AC 2[17]; **Atk** bite (1d8 + poison) and coils (2d6 + constrict); **Move** 15; **Save** 8; **AL** N; **CL/XP** 10/1400; **Special:** constrict (automatic 2d6 damage per round after successful coil attack), magic resistance (20%), poison (save or die), spells (as 8th-level caster). (see **Appendix A: New Monsters**)
Spells: 1st—*faerie fire, magic missile;* 2nd—*heat metal, hold person, invisibility, obscuring mist;* 3rd—*fireball, remove curse;* 4th—*charm monster;* 5th—*raise dead.*

5. Carlow

As the trees thin ahead, a small village nestled in lush green hills and surrounded by neatly tended crops is visible several miles ahead. Advancing, the path slowly turns into a well-maintained cobblestone road with hedgerows rise alongside it. Carlow's center is set around a crossroads lined with a dozen thatch-roofed houses and business, notably an inn and tavern, a cobbler, a blacksmith, a baker, and a general goods store. A fountain gurgles in the small square in the center of town, and well-tended flower bushes can be seen around the village. A rhythmic *tap-tap-tapping* and *clang* of metal provides a steady rhythm as you approach the tavern. Several large tables are set out front.

These table are empty before lunch, have 1d4 patrons in the afternoons, and 2d6 patrons in the evenings.

5-A. The Red Shoe

A wooden sign showing signs of recent touchups hangs above the door of this thatch-roofed stone building with a wattle-and-daub second story showing exposed beams. A wooden flowerbox sprouts red and gold tulips below a wide bay window with several well-crafted pairs of shoes, including a pair of supple high-calf brown leather boots with a gleaming brass buckle, a pair of ankle-height red leather shoes with golden buttons and clasps, and a pair of sturdy black leather shoes meant for a child. The interior of the shop is cluttered and dark but cozy. A large workbench contains scraps of leather, wooden soles of various sizes, nails and brads, and a pair of well-cared-for tools. A short man with wild brown hair, a pair of brass spectacles, and a brown leather apron carefully taps, nailing leather to the sole of a shoe.

Leath Brogan is a soft-spoken man who always has a slightly manic smile on his face. He calls out to anyone who enters and takes a moment to get his work to a point where he may successfully pause. He is highly regarded as the finest cobbler in the area. One can spend nearly as much as is desired on a pair of shoes here, but a sturdy pair of reliable shoes can be had for 2 sp. Custom work with fine leathers and expensive adornments can run as much as 250 gp. Leath always has about a dozen pairs of shoes prepared in a variety of common sizes. They range in price from 2 sp to 28 gp. Leath is transformed into the mythical Luricawne spoken of later that night in the Seanche's cursed song.
Leath Brogan, Male Human Cobbler: HP 5; **AC** 9[10]; **Atk** weapon (1d6); **Move** 12; **Save** 18; **AL** N; **CL/XP** B/10; **Special:** none. (*Monstrosities* 254)

5-B. Wizard's Weal Tavern

Roughly hewn wooden tables and benches sit in front of this two-story stone building with a thatch roof. Your eyes are immediately drawn to the bronze face hung above the door. The interior of the Wizard's Weal is dark with a low ceiling made more precarious with the visible wooden beams. A six-foot span of dark polished wood shows the signs and stains of years of steady use. Several shelves on the wall behind the bar contain bottles of spirits, wine, and liqueurs. Three kegs rest in cradles below the shelves. Small glowing stones are hung about the room and create a soft glow of amber and yellow lights. The man behind the bar is an exceedingly tall elf wearing a purple and black robe with crudely stitched silver stars. His face lights up when he sees you. "I am Findolin! The proprietor of the Wizard's Weal. Might I interest you in one of our arcane alchemical libations? Or have you come to gaze upon the mysterious brazen head?" Findolin gestures to a bronze face set into the stone above the fireplace.

The runes are found to be only facsimiles of "best guesses" of runes or even completely made up symbols that have an arcane feel; in other words, they are fakes. Findolin regularly makes flawed attempts to sound wise and wizardly, and is quick to offer his newest "elixir" or concoction created from mixing his large collection of spirits and liqueurs with seeming randomness. He often attempts to entice customers with the newest item he has muddled for a drink, and the items are often surprising or food adjacent, like soil that grew a rare variety of mushroom.

The Brazen Head

The bronze face, or brazen head, is approximately three feet wide and four feet long. The face is a man with an aquiline nose, thick curly beard, and high cheekbones. He wears a cowl with intricate patterns decorating the edges. If a *detect magic* is used, the face radiates a steady aura of magic. The face may be activated by using an action to speak command words while placing an offering in its mouth.

There are two commands for the face. Both of the command words needed to activate the brazen head are etched into the bar glasses. A beer can be obtained for 5 cp and once it is finished, the command words "slainte chugaibh" (*slawn-cha hoo-uv*, "health to you [all]") are seen carefully etched into the glass. A glass of whiskey can be ordered for 1 gp, and the bottom of this glass proclaims, "slainte agus tainte" (*slawn-cha ogg-uss tawn-cheh*, "health and wealth").

The face accepts offerings to empower itself. If someone is boosted to its mouth, it opens and a flat bronze tongue grinds out, waiting. Placing gemstones, coins, or enchanted items on the tongue and speaking the command words activate the face.

It has the ability to:
- Answer a question regarding any event that occurs in the next seven days within 50 miles using a short phrase or sentence. This costs 25 gp worth of valuable items that can be fit into the brazen head's mouth. There is no limit to the number of times this may be used, and it is always successful.
- Answer any yes or no question. This power has a cumulative 10% failure rate each time it is used. For example, the first try has a 0% chance of failure, the second has a 10% chance, the third a 20% chance, and so on. A failure results in no answer. This costs 75 gp worth of valuables that can be fit into the brazen head's mouth.

The brazen head has always been an object of wonder in this village, and some believe the tavern and village grew up around it. The locals believe that it protects and blesses them. They tell a story about how it commanded a swindling peddler to leave the village in a booming voice with cracks of thunder, darkening clouds, and flashes of lightning. In truth, this item was created more than 900 years ago by the wizard Mor Kegan to demonstrate to her on again, off again partner what a useful man looked like. Since then, it has been involved in predicting several curses, forewarning precipitous calamities, and revealing the location of a grand treasure.

The Seanche in Carlow

The Seanche enters Carlow on the fourth day of the adventure. If the characters are present that evening, they enjoy the following encounter:

When the Seanche enters Carlow, he heads to the Wizard's Weal and trades his musical talents for a drink, a meal, and a spot in the stables overnight. He tunes and begins his set with several rowdy ballads and requests from the audience, which quickly grows in size once the townsfolk hear him performing.

His performance is exceptional and ends with a rollicking tale of a little man in a red vest and red tricorn hat. The man was the finest cobbler in the area. An ugly, squat, fey creature with a round face known as Luricawne wagered the little man that he was a better cobbler. Both of these skilled craftsmen worked all night, tapping away at soles, stretching leather, attaching buttons and clasps. But when it was over, the little man in the red vest was clearly the winner. Luricawne was angry but handed the little man the gold he had wagered and then said, "Your shoes are so fine, they make their own music." After this, the cobbler began boasting to everyone about his skill and about how he was a better cobbler than even mystical creatures. This angered Luricawne when he heard it, so he hatched a plan. He toiled for nine days and nine nights and built perhaps the finest shoe hammer ever crafted. It was silver and etched with scrolling leaf work. Despite its tremendous delicacy, it struck with the force of a much larger hammer, driving a nail into the sole of a shoe in a single tap.

Luricawne left the hammer on the door of the cobbler with a note that read, "The finest tool for the finest cobbler. May all your shoes be good enough to dance in!" The cobbler was overjoyed and immediately began making shoes with the hammer. After nearly a month of building the finest shoes for his neighbors, the full moon rose, and with it, the shoes awoke. They sought out the feet of their masters and took them dancing into the moonlight. Most people awoke the next day confused, in strange places, and with extremely sore feet. From that day forward, the cobbler was ruined, and nobody wanted his fabulous dancing shoes.

Roll 1d6 on the table below and add +1 for each character who succeeds on a saving throw:

1d6	Effect Noticed
1–4	There is something magical about this tune.
5–7	The effect is not influencing people but it is drawing something from them.
8+	The effect of the magic emanating from the lute and this man's voice is drawing some power or lifeforce in small portions from everyone in the crowd.

The music doesn't cause any lasting damage but anyone who failed the previous saving throw feels exhausted the next day (−1 to hit and damage).

The next morning, anyone in the village who is wearing shoes made by Leath Brogan must make a saving throw or be forced to dance. The villagers begin dancing their way to the town's center where Leath Brogan has transformed into a caricature of his former self clad all in red: a physical manifestation of Luricawne. He sets up his lair in the center of town, which becomes a dancefloor of madness and chaos.

If the characters arrive in Carlow after the Seanche, read or paraphrase the following:

The battle begins after this welcome into the impromptu lair of the cursed Leath Brogan in his **Luricawne** form. The dancers are unwilling participants; some are sobbing or crying, and others appear to be furious. There are 30 dancers who surround and protect the Luricawne. They circle around him in kick lines and lash out at any enemies who come within range.

Luricawne: HD 8; **HP** 54; **AC** 7[12]; **Atk** strike (1d8) or ranged strike (1d6); **Move** 12; **Save** 8; **AL** C; **CL/XP** 11/1700; **Special:** change partners (3/day, can instantly switch places with a creature within 50ft, save avoids swap), feel the rhythm (3/day, 3 targets within 40ft, save or spend 1d4+2 rounds dancing), immune to charm or sleep, new kicks (3/day, successful strike places *Luricawne shoes* on target, save avoids).

Dancers, Male and Female Humans (30): HP 1d6; **AC** 9[10]; **Atk** kick line (2d6, save for half); **Move** 12; **Save** 18; **AL** Any; **CL/XP** B/10; **Special:** kick line (all creatures wearing *Luricawne shoes* kick enemies, 2d6 damage, save for half). (*Monstrosities* 254)

Note: All of these dancers are being forced to defend the Luricawne. Killing them outright should be considered an evil act.

6. WICKLOW

6-A. FENLAUGH FISH

This is a large rectangular building with double doors toward the docks for loading and processing fresh fish as they come off the boats. The fish is salted and preserved and sold fresh in a small storefront facing the square. **Fineas Fenlaugh** (*fin-ee-us fen-low*) is the fifth Fenlaugh to run this business, and his family has worked for generations processing the fish that the locals harvest. He is a short man, barely crossing five feet, and is nearly as wide. One of the first things that people notice are his wide, thick-fingered hands crisscrossed with faint scars from years filleting fish. One can acquire a day's worth of salted fish for 4 cp.

Fineas Fenlaugh, Male Human Fishmonger: HP 4; **AC** 9[10]; **Atk** hook (1d4); **Move** 12; **Save** 18; **AL** N; **CL/XP** B/10; **Special:** none. (*Monstrosities* 254)

6-B. THE SMART SALMON

Bradan Feasa (*brothan fah-sa*), the Smart Salmon, was named in reference to the deeds of Finn mac Cumhaill (*Finn McCool*).

Anyone who visits the tavern leaves with the heavy smell of fried foods trapped in their clothing. The tavern is also known for serving citrusy white ale that pairs perfectly with the fresh fried cuts of fish. A plate and an ale costs 2 sp. **Grace**, the barkeep, is a woman in her late 20s with a temper as fiery as it is fast. She's been known to snap at a drunken fool and shift to the sweetest and most inviting proprietress a moment later. She can often be heard arguing with her sister, **Anne**, whose own mercurial temper is more than a match for Grace's.

Grace, Female Human Barkeep: HP 3; **AC** 9[10]; **Atk** club (1d4); **Move** 12; **Save** 18; **AL** N; **CL/XP** B/10; **Special:** none. (*Monstrosities* 254)

Anne, Female Human Barkeep: HP 4; **AC** 9[10]; **Atk** dagger (1d4); **Move** 12; **Save** 18; **AL** N; **CL/XP** B/10; **Special:** none. (*Monstrosities* 254)

THE SEANCHE IN WICKLOW

If the characters arrive before the Seanche, the town is exuberant, excited by the discovery of a silvery shoal of salmon.

The villagers are all busy working in the square, cleaning and filleting the catch before it is either salted or sent to the smokers. A small crowd of people is laughing and ending their labors as teenage boys and girls circulate among them with tankards of ale. As the local cats begin moving in, others rinse the square with buckets of saltwater and stiff-bristled brushes. The crowd drifts toward the tavern. The Seanche arrives in the early evening of the fifth night of the adventure as the party is really beginning in earnest. He enters the town playing his pipes, bringing music that seems to match and enhance the mood of this spontaneous celebration. He sings numerous songs of the sea, of loss, of treasures, or of fantastic creatures.

But the song he ends his night with tells a tale of a fisherman who murdered the wife of the King of Pikes. The King of Pikes then began sinking the ships from the fisherman's village, demanding that the fisherman give the king his wife. With a heavy heart, the village offered the fisherman's wife to the pike. At the last minute, the fisherman's wife turned to the pike and asked if he would not take her murderous husband instead. The pike did not have to think very long before it leapt from the water and snatched the fisherman up into its jaws before disappearing into the dark, choppy waters. With that, the Seanche retires to the stables for the evening and once again disappears early in the morning when the world is still waking or perhaps after the fishermen set out before the rest of the world rises.

Roll 1d6 on the table below and add +1 for each character who succeeds on a saving throw:

1d6	Effect Noticed
1–4	There is something magical about this tune.
5–7	The effect is not influencing people but it is drawing something from them.
8+	The effect of the magic emanating from the lute and this man's voice is drawing some power or lifeforce in small portions from everyone in the crowd.

The music doesn't cause any lasting damage but anyone who failed the previous saving throw feels exhausted the next day (−1 to hit and damage).

The next day, the fishing fleet returns at midday in small groups. As they jockey into position and beginning mooring themselves, a shout goes up. A character has a 4-in-6 chance to spot a long, large, dark shape in the waters below the ships. It looks to be about 40 feet long. In a splash of water and an explosion of wood, a huge pike crests the water and snatches one of the fishermen into its jaws before smashing its way through the ship and back into the dark, obscuring depths. The fishermen immediately abandon their ships by jumping from ship to ship until they reach shore.

The **giant pike** leaps across ships and attempts to grab a creature and carry it into the water. The water below the ships and near the docks is only 30 feet deep at this time. The giant pike targets a fisherman or anyone who causes it harm. It attacks each round it can while maneuvering closer to the largest groups of prey. If it happens to devour a woman, it leaves, placated. While the pike attacks, the fishermen on the farthest ship out frantically draw in their trawling net. The net is still spread from the ship to the ocean floor. Tangled in this net is the giant pike's wife, an equally enormous and thickly muscled giant pike. This pike snaps at anyone who approaches. If she is freed, both pikes join each other and leave the area.

Giant Pikes (2): HD 11; HP 80 (male), 65 (female); AC 3[16]; **Atk** bite (3d6), tail slap (2d6); **Move** 18 (swim) or 30ft leap; **Save** 4; **AL** N; **CL/XP** 11/1700; **Special:** swallow (natural 20 to hit, 2d6 damage per round). (see **Appendix A: New Monsters**)

The Emerald Plains

Before you is the aptly named Emerald Plains, a rich and rolling farmland filled with lush pastures, stands of tall straight trees, and crops neatly trimmed with tall hedges. To the northeast, Bru Na Brighid, Brighid's Tomb, can be seen, bearing its crafted stone bones to the sky as it rises from the underworld. To the south is Tabla An-Mohr, the Giant's Table, a plateau of pale gray stones. The top is stacked with piles of rock formations that create networks and pockets of caverns colloquially known as the Giant's Feast. Located directly to the east, a glimmering blue lake breaks the otherwise green rolling landscape. The Hartwood, the largest stand of trees in the plains, is directly west. Even from this distance, a glimmering silver tree can be seen standing far above the trees that surround it. To the north, the bountiful land breaks into a rocky shoreline of deep blue waters with several groups of buildings interspersed.

A glint of emerald can be detected among the rocks of the Giant's Table. At this point, it is advisable to share the area map with the characters. Allow them to see the various points of interest spread out on the map. The characters can explore the plains in any order they wish, but they inevitably encounter signs of the Seanche and the effects of his curse. Keep track of travel times because the timeline and path of the Seanche are denoted in the map and the characters may encounter him again. The Seanche's path leads to the center of the Hartwood where his final confrontation with Gnaddr occurs.

7. Tabla An-Mohr

The time of day drastically affects the appearance and environment of Tabla An-Mohr. During the nights or if the weather is extremely cold, very few signs of life can be found among the stacks of rocks on this windswept plateau. During the day, the area has traffic like that of a small city, albeit all of the travelers are various types of serpents. None of the serpents encountered is aggressive. The slopes of the plateau are steep inclines piled with loose shale and soil. Non-thief characters have a 25% chance to climb the steep slope of the plateau; three successful checks are needed to complete the climb. Fortunately, failure just results in an embarrassing and dusty slide to the bottom with boots full of dirt. If the characters fail and become frustrated, several local snakes notice their troubles and offer to assist them up the slope. These giant snakes allow the characters to cling to their tails.

7-A. The Giant's Feast Cave formations

1. Rock Pile

This stack of rocks radiates the heat of the sun both day and night. A low and wide cavern entrance gapes like an open mouth into a 10-foot drop into a roughly circular 15-foot-wide chamber. The chamber is warm and dark but movement across the floor is immediately apparent even in the dark lighting. At night, **1d4 + 8 swarms of poisonous snakes** rest in the cavern. During the day, **1d3 + 1 swarms of poisonous snakes** are inside. In the midst of the snakes are three ornately decorated urns. The urns contain 161 gp, 317 sp, 339 sp, and a pair of silver raven earrings with topaz eyes.
Swarms of Poisonous Snakes (1d4+8 [night] or 1d3+1 [day]): HD 2; AC 5[14]; **Atk** bite (1d6 + poison); **Move** 18; **Save** 18; **AL** N; **CL/XP** 2/30; **Special:** poison (+2 save or die).

2. Cave Entrance

The entrance to this cavern system is tall and thin and may present problems for characters trying to enter while wearing heavy armor. The cavern immediately begins to rise and widens against a rough cliff with numerous handholds available. The cliff rises 20 feet to a low and wide ledge that is about three feet high. It is possible to crawl forward to where the path branches into a fork, with the left path rising and the right path descending. The left path leads to a 15-foot-by-10-foot cave with a small opening onto a sunny ledge. This is the lair of several juvenile emerald nagas, and they are always present at night. There is a 3-in-10 chance that **2 juvenile emerald nagas** are present during the day. Disturbing them alerts the other snakes in the area. The path to the right descends to a large 30-foot-by-20-foot rough-walled natural cavern. The floor is littered with bones, rusted weapons, worn equipment, and tattered clothing. Lounging about the cavern during the night are **5 swarms of poisonous snakes**. During the day, only 3 swarms of poisonous snakes are present.
Emerald Nagas (Juvenile) (2): HD 5; HP 36, 31; AC 5[14]; **Atk** bite (1d6 + poison) and coils (1d6 + constrict); **Move** 12; **Save** 12; **AL** N; **CL/XP** 5/240; **Special:** constrict (automatic 1d6 damage per round after successful coil attack), magic resistance (10%), poison (save or die). (see **Appendix A: New Monsters**)
Swarms of Poisonous Snakes (5 [night] or 3 [day]): HD 2; AC 5[14]; **Atk** bite (1d6 + poison); **Move** 18; **Save** 18; **AL** N; **CL/XP** 2/30; **Special:** poison (+2 save or die).

3. Cave

This cave has the most inviting entrance of all of the rock formations that make up the Giant's Feast. It can be seen from most of the plateau. A 30-foot-wide and 15-foot-tall entrance opens into an enormous cavern with a ceiling dotted with stalactites and a floor littered with stalagmites. A musky scent with hints of cloying sweetness accompanies the litter of snakeskins that fill the room. The only clear spot in the room is a bubbling pool that steams with heat. During the daytime, this room is empty. At night, **10 swarms of poisonous snakes** are here. The pool that warms the room is superheated by a **fire elemental** trapped in a cold-iron cage. The cage is a six-inch ball of iron bands cut deeply with runes. It is cold to the touch despite being surrounded by the searing heat the angry elemental is pouring out. The fire elemental may escape its prison with a casting of *dispel magic* (against a 12th-level caster). The fire elemental is quite upset about having been trapped and is immediately aggressive toward any nearby creatures.
Swarms of Poisonous Snakes (10 [night]): HD 2; AC 5[14]; **Atk** bite (1d6 + poison); **Move** 18; **Save** 18; **AL** N; **CL/XP** 2/30; **Special:** poison (+2 save or die).
Fire Elemental: HD 8; HP 55; AC 2[17]; **Atk** strike (3d8); **Move** 12; **Save** 8; **AL** N; **CL/XP** 9/1100; **Special:** +1 or better magic weapons to hit, ignite materials (save to resist). (***Monstrosities*** 156)

4. The Main Dish

This rock formation dwarfs the other "dishes" present in the Giant's Feast and is clearly the main course. A wide cavern entrance shows that the cavern network immediately branches into three paths:
4a. This path wends its way around to the left for 35 feet before ending in a 10-foot-wide clearing. About 15 feet from the end of the passage, a crunching sound can be heard with each step, and snakeskins are piled several layers deep across the floor. At night, a **juvenile emerald naga** rests here. There is a 3-in-10 chance that it is present during daylight hours.
Emerald Naga (Juvenile): HD 5; HP 30; AC 5[14]; **Atk** bite (1d6 + poison) and coils (1d6 + constrict); **Move** 12; **Save** 12; **AL** N; **CL/XP** 5/240; **Special:** constrict (automatic 1d6 damage per round after successful coil attack), magic resistance (10%), poison (save or die). (see **Appendix A: New Monsters**)

4b. This passage slopes gently downward for 40 feet before opening into a wide, low-ceilinged chamber with rough natural walls. Swinging a sword or melee weapon is difficult with the low ceiling (–2 to hit and damage). Piles of coins and gems are strewn about the room, and careful observation detects emerald green scales among the piles. This chamber is the sleeping quarters of the queen of the emerald serpents (see **Area 7-B**).

4c. This narrow tunnel is about three feet wide and high, with a floor smoothed from regular travel. It stretches 15 feet before turning sharply to the right and continues for another 10 feet before opening into a roughly rectangular chamber 40 feet long by 30 feet wide. Interspersed along the sides of the cavern are eight 10-foot-wide pits in the floor.
Pit 1: Slowly pacing in the bottom of this pit is an elegantly dressed man who exudes fey charm. Despite being stuck in a pit, his fine clothing is spotless, and he appears relaxed. The **summer knight** addresses anyone who approaches the edge of the pit and looks at him. He demands to know what the characters are gawking at. He also informs them that despite being bored, he is not so bored that he would deign to speak with them. Of course, he continues to speak with the characters.

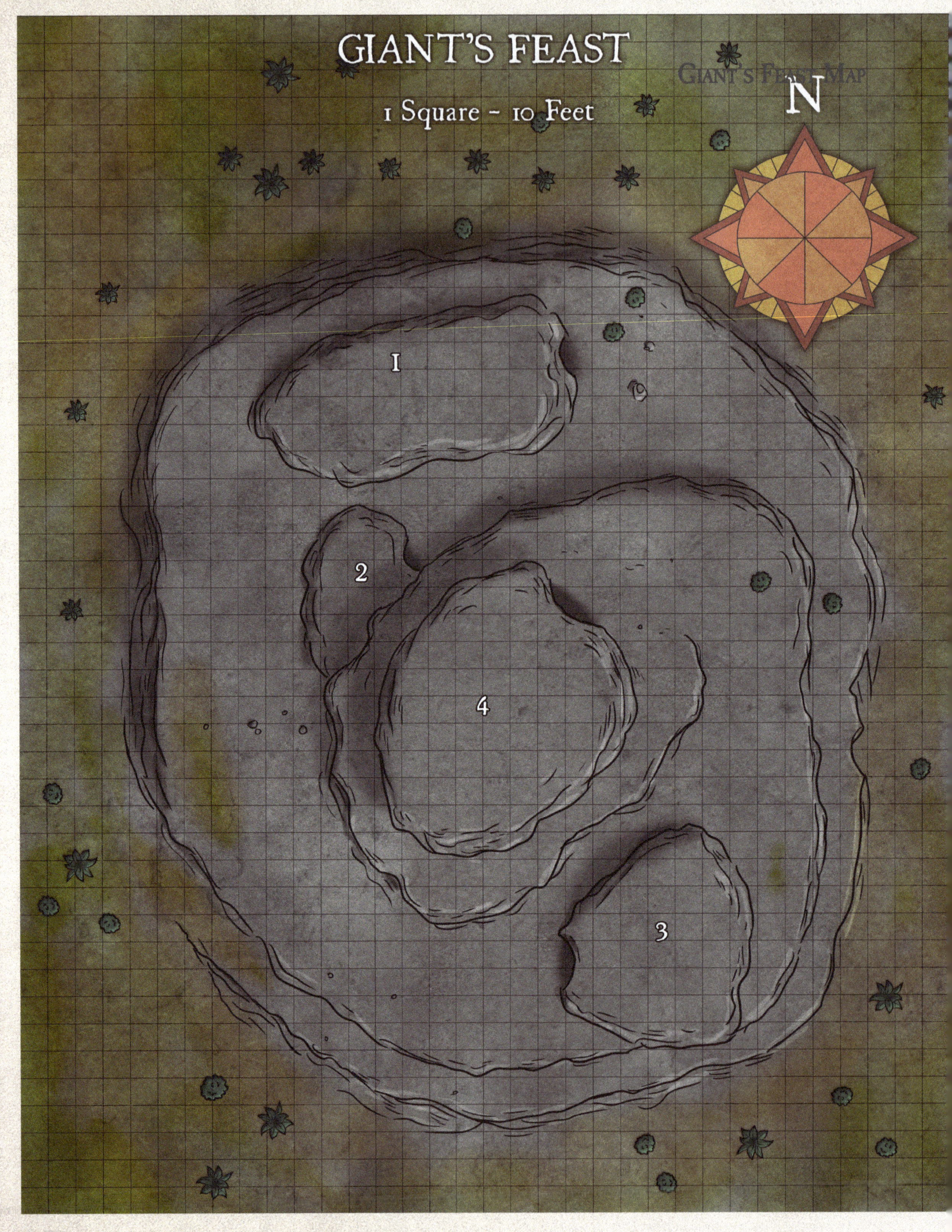

GIANT'S FEAST
1 Square – 10 Feet
Giant's Feast Map
N
1
2
4
3

He has the following information that he imparts to those willing to listen to his egotistical conversation:

1. This fey lord introduces himself as a knight of summer. He was sent by the Tuatha De Danann to return Gnaddr to his home plane. The queen of the emerald serpents imprisoned him here.
2. He is stuck in this realm until Gnaddr returns to his home plane; he is magically anchored to him.
3. Of course he could escape if he wanted. The queen knows this, too. He says he told her that "he would not initiate an escape."
4. The queen is a potential ally in stopping Gnaddr, but she is currently limited and bound by a deal she made with Gnaddr.
5. A smith in the Lazy Lake may be willing to aid the characters if they attempt to stop Gnaddr.

> The man in the pit looks you over and says, "I have given the emerald queen my word that I will not leave here through my own power. But I have not given her my parole. I wish you well if you are trying to stop Gnaddr, and I would help you if I could."

The summer knight is hinting that he is able to aid the characters, but he is unable to affect his own escape or to assist in it.

Summer Knight: HD 10; HP 63; AC 3[16]; **Atk** weapon (1d8); **Move** 12; **Save** 5; **AL** L; **CL/XP** 12/2000; **Special:** magic resistance (10%), nature's grace (3/day, 60ft radius, cause green tendril to bloom healing pollen, heal 3d6 damage), vulnerable to iron (200% damage). (see **Appendix A: New Monsters**)

Pit 2: This pit drops 20 feet and opens into a 30-foot-wide chamber. It contains a withered and long-dead body wrapped in the rotted clothes in which it expired. A beautiful gleaming short sword still rests against the fingertips of the corpse, and several jeweled rings are on its bony fingers. The body is the mortal coil of an **ekimmu** trapped in this cell. A character who carefully examines the pit has a 2-in-6 chance to spot a thin rail of silver cut into the wall below the lip of the pit. The silver ribbon is scrawled with a script that does not seem to have a beginning or an end. The silver is evidence of ritual magic used to trap the ekimmu, and it blocks the ekimmu from escaping the cell. The barrier that stops the ekimmu does not prevent a living being from entering or leaving. If the script is damaged or destroyed, the ekimmu is free to use its malevolence ability to immediately affect anyone in range. The ekimmu waits until the characters steal its former possessions before it materializes out of the body and surprises them with a paralyzing howl. The magical short sword is named *Deadly Whisper* (see **Appendix B: New Magic Items**), and the rings are worth 275 gp, 130 gp, and 35 gp.

Ekimmu: HD 8; HP 52; AC 3[16]; **Atk** touch (3d4); **Move** 0 (fly 12); **Save** 8; **AL** N; **CL/XP** 10/1400; **Special:** malevolence (1/round, can possess and control target, as *magic jar*, save avoids), paralyzing howl (3/day, 30ft radius, save or paralyzed for 1d4+1 rounds), rejuvenate (returns in 2d6 days). (see **Appendix A: New Monsters**)

Pit 3: This pit is a straight 20-foot drop, but after five feet nearly-clear crystals of ice coat the walls and floor to create a scintillating kaleidoscope of colors that is nearly mesmerizing. Any creature who descends more than five feet into the pit must make a saving throw. On a failed save, they take 2d6 points of cold damage. On a successful save, they take half this amount.

Pit 4: The interior of this 30-foot-deep pit appears to be constructed of rough tree bark, as though someone had turned a tree inside out. Small branches, unable to support significant weight, jut out of the sides with regularity. The bottom of the pit is filled with a pale jade green liquid. A creature who touches the liquid must make a saving throw. On a failed saving throw, its movement is halved as the creature begins to grow bark. The creature must make another saving throw at the beginning of its next turn. A creature who fails three saves becomes a petrified statue of bark for 24 hours. A creature who succeeds on any of the saving throws ends the effects and is immune to the liquid for 24 hours.

Pit 5: The interior of this 20-foot-deep pit is coated with iron plates riveted to the floor and walls. The walls of this pit are coated with an enchanted cold iron that deals 1d8 points of damage to any fey creature that touches it. A five-foot wooden dais rises from the center. An ornate wooden chair with a back splat limned with leaf-like carvings continues into relief carvings that extend down the legs into ball and claw feet. The wood itself is a rich red mahogany seemingly flecked with gold. The chair has been polished into a high glossy sheen.

Pit 6: This pit descends six feet to a dark liquid pool as still as glass. Despite the thirst for light this liquid exhibits, intelligent creatures are reflected in the pool. Anyone touching the liquid must make a saving throw. On a failed save, the liquid begins to coat their body wherever they touched it and they suffer 1d8 points of damage and are held in place. On a successful save, they suffer half this damage and are not held. A held creature takes 1d8 points of damage at the beginning of each of its turns.

Pit 7: This pit is only 10 feet deep, and the walls and floor are covered in irregular rock formations. Anyone observing the rock for 12 or more seconds has a 3-in-6 chance to notice that the rock here is moving slightly, perhaps as if it is breathing. If loud noises are made or if the rock floor or walls are touched, a single saucer-sized eye slowly opens and observes the area. This creature is an **elemental adder (stone)**.

Q'rack, the elemental adder, attacks anyone attempting to free a prisoner. He does not do anything if the ekimmu is disturbed. He is the guardian of the cells. As long as the characters have SS'Thissk's permission, he does not disturb them as they explore this area.

Q'rack, Elemental Adder (Earth/Stone): HD 9; HP 66; AC 3[16]; **Atk** bite (1d6), tail smash (2d4); **Move** 15; **Save** 6; **AL** N; **CL/XP** 10/1400; **Special:** avalanche (3/day, 30ft line, 3d6 damage, save for half), immune to slashing and piercing weapons. (see **Appendix A: New Monsters**)

Pit 8: This 15-foot-deep pit has a bare stone floor and walls covered in what seems to be thousands of skulls. A character can determine that these skulls range in age from several months to hundreds of years. The species of the skulls is quite diverse and ranges from beast to humanoid, including a cyclops, several with lizard or draconic features, and creatures with canine and feline features. The skulls react whenever they see an intelligent creature. If they notice anyone, a great number of them begin attempting to speak to the closest creature in a variety of languages. Anyone hearing the voices must make a saving throw or be affected as if by a *confusion* spell. A failure means that this character stands confused and cannot identify a single voice and may not cast any spell. The skulls do not stop speaking until they do not detect anyone. A creature within five feet of the skulls when inside the pit is bitten by 1d6 skulls. The skulls attack as 4 HD creatures and do 1d4 points of damage each.

7-B. The Queen of the Emerald Serpents

During the day, **SS'Thissk**, an **emerald naga queen**, lounges upon the tallest piles of rocks on the plateau. She enjoys the heat of the sun and the expansive view of the lands around her. Her body scintillates with hues of green and casts strange, liquid-like shadows that ripple and move. Her coiled body seems to stretch 20 feet and ends in a perfectly shaped and comely green-skinned humanoid face. She wears a simple, supple, honey-brown leather halter with several small pouches. She always rests alongside or atop **4 giant constrictor snakes** that accompany her everywhere she goes. There are also **3 juvenile emerald nagas** nearby enjoying the sun shining on their sparkling green scales. If SS'Thissk is approached in a friendly manner — perhaps with a gift recognizing her authority as the queen of the emerald serpents — she listens and shares information. It benefits her if the characters deal with Gnaddr because it frees her of the *geased* deal that traps her and her family on this plane. She desires nothing more than to return home, especially with the treasure she thought she had tricked from Gnaddr. If the characters persuade her to help, they may gain some assistance. Feel free to add pluses or minuses to the roll based on how the characters interact with the naga queen. Roll 1d6 on the table below to see what she provides:

1d6	Boon
1	No assistance
2–3	*Potion of healing*
4	*Restorative ointment*
5	*Potion of greater healing*
6	All potions listed above

The queen also shares the following information with the characters:
- Gnaddr and his minions are vulnerable to weapons wrought from the cold iron obtained from a fallen star.
- Although he may seem alone, Gnaddr always has a retinue of creatures protecting him. The queen has seen him most often with a pack of wolf-like creatures from his home plane. These creatures heal themselves if they aren't silenced.
- The Lazy Lake is known for its puissant arms. If asked to elaborate, the queen seems surprised that the characters haven't found arms in lakes before.

SS'Thissk, Emerald Naga (Queen): HD 10; HP 76; AC 2[17]; **Atk** bite (1d8 + poison) and coils (2d6 + constrict); **Move** 15; **Save** 5; **AL** N; **CL/XP** 12/2000; **Special:** constrict (automatic 2d6 damage per round after successful coil attack), magic resistance (30%), phase strike (1/day, 50ft radius, 3d6 damage and knocked prone, save for half and avoid being knocked prone), poison (save or die), spells (as 10th-level caster). (see **Appendix A: New Monsters**)
Spells: 1st—*faerie fire, magic missile;* 2nd—*heat metal, hold person, invisibility, obscuring mist;* 3rd—*fireball, remove curse;* 4th—*charm monster;* 5th—*raise dead.*

Emerald Nagas (Juveniles) (3): HD 5; HP 34, 30, 24; AC 5[14]; **Atk** bite (1d6 + poison) and coils (1d6 + constrict); **Move** 12; **Save** 12; **AL** N; **CL/XP** 5/240; **Special:** constrict (automatic 1d6 damage per round after successful coil attack), magic resistance (10%), poison (save or die). (see **Appendix A: New Monsters**)

Giant Constrictors (4): HD 6; HP 43, 37, 35, 29; AC 5[14]; **Atk** bite (1d3), constrict (2d4); **Move** 10; **Save** 11; **AL** N; **CL/XP** 7/600; **Special:** constrict (automatic 2d4 damage after hit; 1-in-6 chance to pin limb). (***Monstrosities** 440)

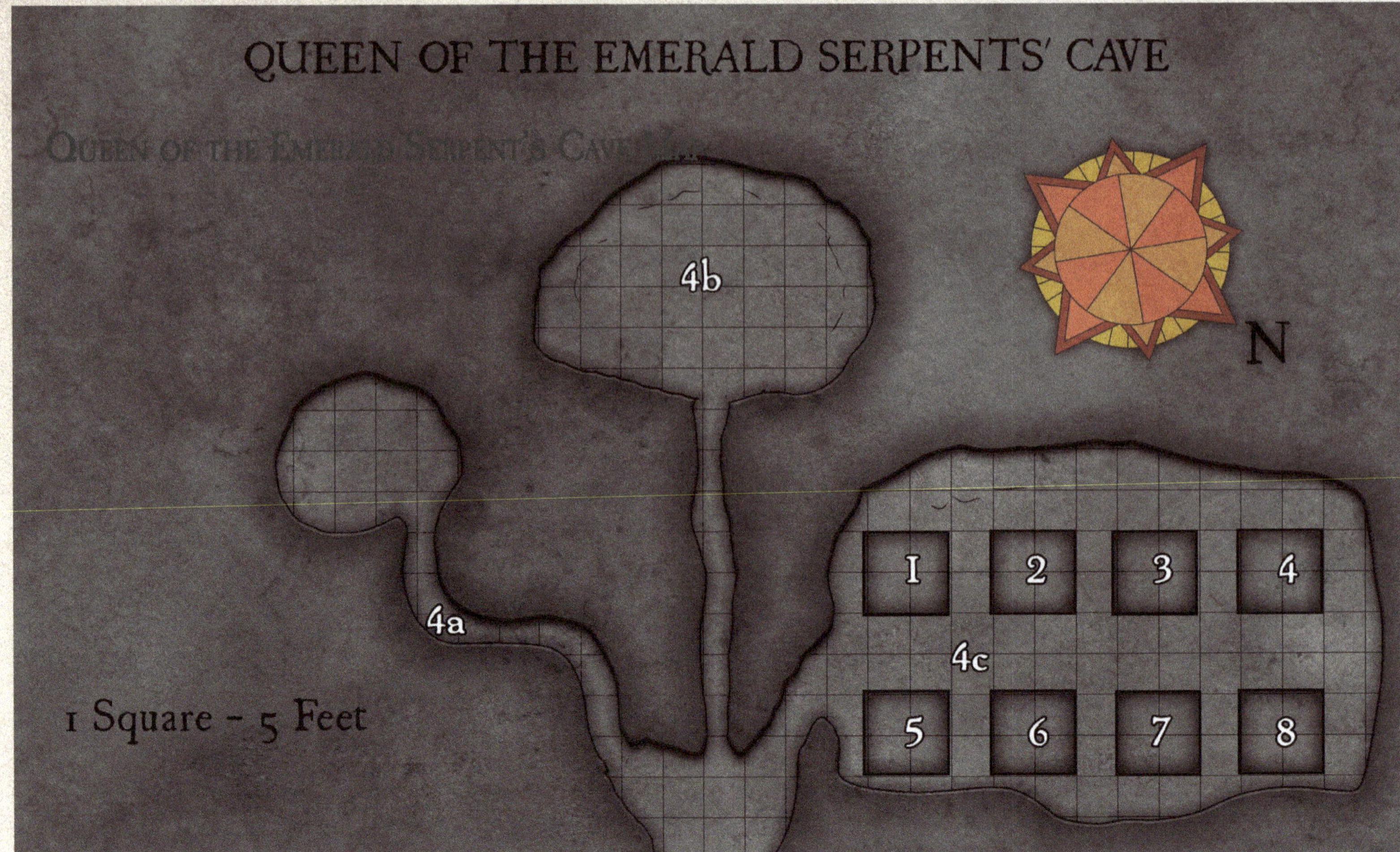

8. BRU NA BRIGHID

A round-topped hill obscures a view of the sea behind it. Its waist is covered in lush green grass, and a stone structure emerges from the rich soil. The structure is built from large, roughly worked stones, and several entrances lead into it from each cardinal direction. Several small buildings are built around the base of the wide low hill, and people can be seen moving about from a distance. If the hill is observed for most of a day, people are likely observed climbing up and into the structure.

An inn with a tavern, a general goods store, and several homes are clustered near a path leading to the top of the hill. The path is well worn and clearly maintained. Neat lines of rocks mark the edges and the beginning of the path. Candles are placed upon flattish stones every six to 10 feet and on some evenings they are lit, wending a twinkling path to the shrine that rises from the hill.

When the characters enter the village, a commotion can be heard. Snakes cover the ground outside the window and around the buildings and on the road. The small snakes swarming the ground are not the most disturbing thing, however; that would be the brightly glimmering emerald snake stretching more than 10 feet long with an exquisite woman's face. She is followed by three smaller yet similar snake creatures with the faces of teenage girls. This group of serpents consists of an **emerald naga**, **3 juvenile emerald nagas**, and **5 swarms of poisonous snakes**. They are moving through the village, with some of the smaller snakes eating and killing small, domesticated animals. The nagas seem to be herding the snakes and attempting to move them through the village as quickly as possible. If the nagas are unmolested, they respectfully nod to the characters and continue herding the snakes away from the cluster of buildings as quickly as they can. If the characters engage the nagas in an aggressive manner, the emerald naga and one of the juvenile emerald nagas attempt to keep the characters busy while the rest of the serpents escape toward Tabla An-Mohr. However the interaction with the nagas goes, the villagers are grateful for the characters' intervention.

Emerald Naga (Adult): HD 8; HP 49; AC 2[17]; Atk bite (1d8 + poison) and coils (2d6 + constrict); **Move** 15; **Save** 8; **AL** N; **CL/XP** 10/1400; **Special:** constrict (automatic 2d6 damage per round after successful coil attack), magic resistance (20%), poison (save or die), spells (as 8th-level caster). (see **Appendix A: New Monsters**)
Spells: 1st—*faerie fire, magic missile*; 2nd—*heat metal, hold person, invisibility, obscuring mist*; 3rd—*fireball, remove curse*; 4th—*charm monster*; 5th—*raise dead*.
Emerald Nagas (Juveniles) (3): HD 5; HP 37, 33, 25; AC 5[14]; Atk bite (1d6 + poison) and coils (1d6 + constrict); **Move** 12; **Save** 12; **AL** N; **CL/XP** 5/240; **Special:** constrict (automatic 1d6 damage per round after successful coil attack), magic resistance (10%), poison (save or die). (see **Appendix A: New Monsters**)

Swarms of Poisonous Snakes (5): HD 2; HP 15, 13x2, 11, 9; AC 5[14]; Atk bite (1d6 + poison); **Move** 18; **Save** 18; **AL** N; **CL/XP** 2/30; **Special:** poison (+2 save or die).

8-A. BRIGHID'S REST

This inn has a stable, six guest rooms, and a cozy tavern that serves flavorful and hearty local cuisine. **Roisin** (*ro-sheen*) runs this tavern with her two teenage boys. Her husband "run off with some trollop years ago." She provides quality service in a clean tavern. She provides a mug of ale and a bowl of stew or shepherd's pie for 6 cp. A heartier spread can be had for 1 sp. She also offers several local ales ranging in quality and price from 1 cp to 1 sp. Her sons **Oisin** (*O-sheen*) and **Darragh** (*Darra*) are hardworking and jovial boys. They are quick to help and just as quick to get into some trouble if they aren't busy. They are often found in the stable playing dice and sipping pilfered ale.

Roisin, Female Human Tavern Owner: HP 3; AC 9[10]; Atk dagger (1d4); **Move** 12; **Save** 18; **AL** N; **CL/XP** B/10; **Special:** none. (*Monstrosities* 254)
Oisin, Male Human Teen: HP 4; AC 9[10]; Atk club (1d4); **Move** 12; **Save** 18; **AL** N; **CL/XP** B/10; **Special:** none. (*Monstrosities* 254)
Darragh, Male Human Teen: HP 5; AC 9[10]; Atk fists (1d2); **Move** 12; **Save** 18; **AL** N; **CL/XP** B/10; **Special:** none. (*Monstrosities* 254)

8-B. SENAN'S SUNDRY SHOP

Senan's shop is housed in a sunflower tallow building with fading blue shutters and a blue door faded at the bottom from years of weather and use. A small brass bell jingles noisily when the door is opened to reveal a shelf-filled room lined with a cluttered countertop. The plethora of items jammed into this store masks the truly useful items. Any mundane equipment can be found here. **Ronan McFarren** is a wiry gentleman wearing a leather apron with pockets stuffed with a variety of tools and trinkets. He is friendly and tries to be helpful, but he is not completely sure what he has in the shop. He purchased the shop from Senan Walsh III, whose family owned the shop for three generations.

Ronan McFarren, Male Human Shopkeeper: HP 2; AC 9[10]; Atk staff (1d6); **Move** 12; **Save** 18; **AL** N; **CL/XP** B/10; **Special:** none. (*Monstrosities* 254)

Ronan has been attempting to court Roisin for several years. He can be found drinking at the tavern or helping the boys with some repair tasks when he isn't in his shop or the apartment above it. Much of his business is in the sale of sacred stones marked with a single rune that are said to grant wishes if dropped into Brighid's Throat within the structure atop the hill. Ronan sells these for 5 cp. He also has several interesting rumors about the area that can be worked into any roleplaying interaction:

- Brighid rode across the sea on a great fiery stallion and collapsed on the hill in a smoldering fire, laying her armor and spear beside her on the stones. She rested on the rocks and entered a shimmering portal the next day dressed in a diaphanous golden gown that floated about her.
- The best fried fish can be found nearby in the village of Wicklow at the Smart Salmon.
- A sea monster has been wrecking all the nets along the coast.

THE SEANCHE IN BRU NA BRIGHID

If the characters arrive during the Seanche's visit to the village (which occurs on the sixth day and seventh night of the adventure), they may see the following:

When the Seanche arrives, he heads to the tavern, as usual. He converses briefly with Roisin and then sets up in a corner near the fire. He chats and spreads local rumors and knowledge and then begins playing. He takes requests for several hours before beginning his cursed song.

The Seanche begins playing a haunting and rhythmic tune, and the room begins to hush. He tells a story about a farmer finding a wrinkled old man in a green vest walking with a shovel on the edge of his property. The little fey man was startled by the farmer, who captured him. The little fey man offered the farmer a deal: If the farmer freed him, he would show him where he buried his gold treasure. The farmer eagerly agreed and found the treasure. He then freed the little fey man and kicked him off his property. The farmer's family became wealthy but were cursed with small annoyances and misfortunes.

The song ends and the crowd appears exhausted as they filter out into the night. The Seanche retires to the stables for the night.

Roll 1d6 on the table below and add +1 for each character who succeeds on a saving throw:

1d6	Effect Noticed
1–4	There is something magical about this tune.
5–7	The effect is not influencing people but it is drawing something from them.
8+	The effect of the magic emanating from the lute and this man's voice is drawing some power or lifeforce in small portions from everyone in the crowd.

The music doesn't cause any lasting damage but anyone who failed the previous saving throw feels exhausted the next day (–1 to hit and damage).

The next day, Ronan and the boys capture a tiny old man in a barrel that they bring into Brighid's Rest. They demand gold from the creature, and poke it with sticks and threaten it.

> "Fine, I'll give ye what ye want," a tinny voice rasps from the barrel.
>
> The boys stop poking with their sticks, and Ronan reaches into the barrel. He pulls a foot-and-a-half tall figure clad in rough-spun brown woolen clothes and shod in brown shoes with burnished gold buckles.
>
> "You swear?" Ronan demands.
>
> "I swear I will take you to the spot I buried those coins but ye don't want them. They're cursed," the little man squeaks seriously.
>
> Ronan plops him onto the ground unceremoniously, and the little man dusts himself off, throwing an angry glare at Ronan. He begins heading just outside of town and into a copse of trees. There, Ronan and the boys dig up an iron cauldron with wooden and leather handles.

The boys and Ronan take the pot to Brighid's Rest and open it to reveal a mound of 50 saucer-sized golden coins. The coins immediately sprout wings and scatter throughout the building and hide until they can make their way back to their true owner. The *leprechaun's gold* (see **Appendix B: New Magic Items**) can be found around the area until all 50 coins are discovered or until two weeks pass.

8-C. BRIGHID'S SHRINE

The worn path leads to the summit of the hill and the stone shrine emerging from it, where it splits to circle the entire summit. At the summit, pea-sized gravel replaces the path. Four entrances lead into the shrine, with one facing each cardinal direction. Another level of dirt and a stone structure rises above the entrance level.

1. MAIN CHAMBER

The main chamber of this structure is 100 feet across and roughly circular. The walls are stone and packed dirt. A staircase cut into the wall along the northwestern wall rises into the ceiling. A 10-foot-wide pit in the center of the shrine falls into a dark chamber. The floor around the pit is worn from years of traffic. A golden statue of Brighid and a golden steed hangs on finely wrought brass chains above the pit, affording clear views of it from up and down the shaft. The wooden statue is covered in gold leaf and is worth 225 gp. However, anyone taking the statue is cursed until they complete three long rests. A cursed creature who rolls a natural 20 on an attack roll must reroll and use the second result.

2. TREASURE PIT

The pit drops onto a pile of small stones in the center of a pool of water. Three islands appear to be empty rises of smooth stone. Crude carvings of boars, sheep, and figures working forges decorate the walls. Each of the islands has a roughly circular spot near the center that is polished and limned in carefully etched glyphs. The characters to discern several of the glyphs and their meaning. The words "light," "protect," "reveal," and "flames" are repeated in each circle. The glyphs of each circle are identical. If the brass shield (**Area 3**) above the pit is polished, light reflected from it strikes the stones and the water below and scatters throughout the entire room to create a bright light that reveals three chests, one in the center of each circle.

One chest contains a bronze spearhead nicked from battle; it awaits only being attached to once again see battle. One chest holds a bronze breastplate that gleams like gold in the sunlight. The final chest contains a much nicer version of the shield that hangs above the shaft. This shield gleams and when lifted, two soft leather bags are found below that contain a figurine of a boar and a ram. See **Appendix B: New Magic Items** for details on *Brighid's raiment and arms*.

3. UPPER CHAMBER

Stairs lead into a narrow and winding passage that rises clockwise to a small chamber built from four wide stone plinths oriented along the cardinal directions. A five-foot-diameter pit in the floor is directly above the pit in the room below. Thin spaces exist in the corners, allowing a character who is small, unarmored, or lightly armored to squeeze through. Mounted into the stone ceiling above the pit is a bronze shield depicting a rising sun. The shield's age is marked with verdigris that gives it a bluish-green hue that nearly matches the sea outside. The shield can be removed from its clips with a little bit of time and elbow grease. If it is polished, it reflects sunlight down into the pit and causes the chests to appear in the treasure pit (**Area 2**).

> ## BRIGHID
>
> In Celtic mythology, Brighid or Brig, is the goddess of spring, health and healing, poetry, fertility, and smithing. She is a member of the Tuatha De Danann and is the daughter of the Dagda, the "father" of Celtic gods. Her feast day is traditionally February 1st and 2nd, which was a pagan festival called Imbolc.
>
> Brighid's temples and shrines are always represented by an eternal flame tended by her priestesses, the Fire Keepers. Her temples and sanctums often contain tools she leaves for the mortals she loves and protects.
>
> Farmers, smiths, soldiers, and other common folk often worship Brighid. Many tales speak of her fearsome and fiery protection touching and affecting the lives of those who worship her.
>
> **Suggested Domains:** Forge, Light, Order
>
> **Tenets:** To protect the family and children. To protect order and peace. To support community.

9. The Lazy Lake

> The blue waters of this lake slap choppily against the lightly wooded shoreline. The lake spreads in a kidney shape several thousand feet across and wide. The water is cool, dark, and fresh.

Searching the shore of the lake reveals several popular fishing spots and a few tree stands for bowhunting. A rocky isle covered in dense, scraggly pines juts from the rough waters near the center of the lake. Getting to the island can be challenging. There are no convenient boats, but a great deal of fallen and fresh trees could easily be fashioned into a raft. The waters of the lake are choppy during the day due to the **8 each-uisce** (*ahk ish keh*) that spend their days playing and running through the waters, creating tumultuous and unpredictable currents. These energetic water horses are playful, which can appear aggressive. They attempt to capsize any vessel that enters the waters so that they may swim and play with the creatures attempting to cross. If a creature truly appears in distress, they bring them to shore. To calm an each-uisce, a character can attempt to gain its attention and favor. This can be done with food or gentle approaches. After this, the each-uisce follows simple commands and transports the character to the island. If attacked, they fight for a few rounds before retreating. They immediately swim away if any of them is killed.

Each-uisce (8): HD 4; **HP** 30, 29, 27, 24x2, 20, 18, 15; **AC** 7[12]; **Atk** kick (1d6); **Move** 15 (swim); **Save** 13; **AL** N; **CL/XP** 4/120; **Special:** resist cold (50% damage), submerge (pull creature underwater with successful melee strike, save or stunned for 1d3 rounds, 1 point damage per round). (see **Appendix A: New Monsters**)

The shores of the isle are quite rocky and irregular, creating numerous small pools and crevasses ideal for hiding abundant life. Thick pines ring the entire isle, and their scratchy needles and sharp branches cause 1d4 points of damage to anyone who simply pushes through them. Moving through at a more cautious pace and cutting branches or using magic makes this task much safer. If magic is used, remember that although these are pine trees, they are fresh and somewhat resistant to bursting into flames. Characters must push through the trees for about 25 feet until they find a clearing with a spring forming a warm, clear pool.

Characters have a 4-in-6 chance to notice a ripple recurring in the center of the pool at regular intervals, and they even hear a dull thud and see a muscular woman swinging a hammer at a red and yellow glowing piece of metal. She looks up and notices the characters observing her. She lifts a hand and waves them down toward her. The water in the pool is warm, like bathwater, but only 15 feet deep. A slightly resistant dome of air forms underwater around the forge and the smith. Crossing into the dome is difficult terrain and anyone entering from the top falls 10 feet to the stone ground of this underwater forge and may take damage. Fish, the each-uisce, and other aquatic animals swim around this dome of air. The smith refuses to help the characters if they killed any each-uisce.

> The forge itself appears to be a well with a metal liner and rim filled with flowing hot magma. Occasionally, the smith dips her sword into the magma, pounds determinedly, and then plunges it into the water that makes up the walls around her forge. The air is humid and smells of old eggs and soot. She places the piece she is working with on a steel bench.
>
> "Greetings! I am the lady of this lake. The land tells me you have dire need." The smith speaks with a rich and melodious voice that carries over the sizzling of heat and water. "If you assist me, I can arm you with the power of this land. This lake was created by a lazy fairy who was busy cavorting with humans rather than maintaining the spring here. Well, a piece of falling iron struck and killed her lover at this very lake. We have time enough to build you a weapon. What is it we should make? A sword? Yes, that will do. What we need to do is this …"

The smith explains the steps of the process and what she needs:

1. "Bring me the metal."

Character must retrieve the meteoric iron from the nearby depression. Unfortunately, the each-uisce love a good game of keep away. They attempt to knock the ore from a character's hands and pass it to each other. A character carrying the meteoric iron must roll 1d6 per hit die opposed by **2 each-uisce** (who together roll 8d6). The winner gets the meteor. A character must succeed at two such checks to successfully bring the ore to the bubble. The each-uisce don't attack unless characters initiate a fight. Even then, they attempt to stun characters by pulling them underwater and then fleeing with the meteor.

Each-uisce (2): HD 4; **HP** 29, 24; **AC** 7[12]; **Atk** kick (1d6); **Move** 15 (swim); **Save** 13; **AL** N; **CL/XP** 4/120; **Special:** resist cold (50% damage), submerge (pull creature underwater with successful melee strike, save or stunned for 1d3 rounds, 1 point damage per round). (see **Appendix A: New Monsters**)

2. "Help me smelt the ore."

Characters must place the iron into the crucible and lower it into the magma until the ore glows a bluish-white. The smith uses a bellows on the magma while she intensely concentrates on the ore. She signals the characters when to remove it.

This requires two characters to lift the bars on each side of the crucible and lower it into the magma to melt. Two consecutive successful saving throws are needed to successfully melt the ore. Both characters involved suffer 1d6 points of fire damage from the heat of the magma. If one or both of them fails, the crucible falls and spills the heated ore, which requires each character to make another saving throw. A character who fails takes 2d6 points of fire damage while one who succeeds takes half this amount.

3. "Help me pour the ore."

Characters must help pour the ore into the mold and safely return the crucible to its cradle while the smith carefully crumbles a glittering whitish powder into the mold.

This portion of the task requires a more delicate hand. To pour the molten ore requires a character to roll below his or her dexterity on 4d6 to add the ore while the smith crumbles some powder into the mold. On a failure, a character must make a saving throw, taking 2d6 points of fire damage on a failure or half as much on a success.

4. "Help me shatter the mold."

Despite how it sounds, shattering the mold actually requires someone to examine the mold and determine the correct spot to strike it. A character who examines the mold must roll below their wisdom on 4d6 to identify the single correct spot to strike the mold to free the gleaming bluish blade. A character must hold a cold chisel while the smith strikes with the hammer. If they select the incorrect spot, the sword shatters, forcing all creatures within the air bubble to make a saving throw. A creature who fails takes 3d6 points of damage while one who succeeds takes half this amount. The smith must begin the process again.

The players are rewarded for their efforts with the *feyslayer sword* (see **Appendix B: New Magic Items**), which can be any type of sword chosen by the characters.

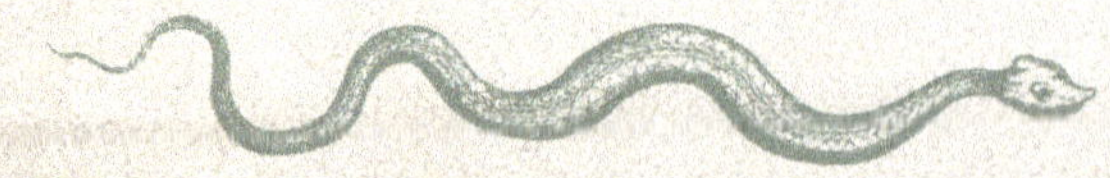

10. The Hartwood

The thick boles create a wall that prevents easy entry into this dark forest. The only visible path is a dark arched tunnel of tree branches over a partially overgrown trail. A yellow and green pavilion tent sits in a grassy area to the side of the road before the forest. It protects a tidy firepit and a wooden plank table covered in white linen and set with silver serving dishes and ewers. Several horses are tethered nearby, and a group of four armored figures with green and gold tabards are completing various chores around the camp. A reed-thin woman with pale jade skin and almond-shaped golden eyes stands nearby. She is clad in scale mail so green it is nearly black. She holds a silver-bladed glaive with a handle of polished ebony. A pair of hand crossbows hang from her belt next to a longsword with a silver pommel and a handle wrapped in black leather.

If the characters approach the woods, one of **Lady Puinseann's men** approaches with his hands held palm forward to invite the characters to join his lady for a drink and brief repast. If they refuse, he calmly returns to his lady and quietly informs her of the characters' decision. At this, **Lady Puinseann** drains her goblet of wine, picks up her glaive, and goes to meet the party in battle in the road with her warriors. Her strategy is to disable any spellcasters while her foot soldiers tie up the melee fighters. Whether or not Gnaddr or the Seanche have arrived, Lady Puinseann attempts to prevent the characters from entering the forest. If they sneak past her, they encounter **12 fey lupes**, and she and her troops join the fight in an attempt to drive the characters away. She even accepts surrender or ceasefire if that becomes an option.

If the characters join her, read or paraphrase the following:

Lady Puinseann attempts to dissuade the characters from entering the woods and interfering with Gnaddr's plans. If they seem insistent, she offers them several items to abandon their plans and leave the Hartwood. She offers a set of *elven chain*, a *cloak of displacement*, and a perfect diamond worth 1,000 gp.

If the characters refuse, she sighs and scans the characters with a resigned look. Read the following:

Combat begins as if the characters had refused her meal as described above.

Lady Puinseann, Female Elf Warrior (Ftr8): HP 56; AC 2[17]; Atk *+1 glaive* (1d8+3 + slow) or longbow x2 (1d6); **Move** 12; **Save** 7; **AL** C; **CL/XP** 8/800; **Special:** +1 to hit and damage strength bonus, darkvision (60ft), detect secret doors, multiple attacks (8) vs. creatures with 1 or fewer HD, vulnerable to iron weapons (200% damage).
  Equipment: plate mail, shield, *+1 glaive* (target slowed [as *slow* spell] with strike, save avoids), longbow, 20 arrows.
  Note: If Lady Puinseann hits with her glaive, the target must make a saving throw or be affected by a *slow* spell.

Lady Puinseann's Men, Male Elf Warriors (Ftr2) (4): HP 12, 10x2, 6; AC 7[12]; **Atk** *longsword* (1d8) or longbow x2 (1d6); **Move** 12; **Save** 13; **AL** C; **CL/XP** 2/30; **Special:** darkvision (60ft), detect secret doors, multiple attacks (2) vs. creatures with 1 or fewer HD.
  Equipment: leather armor, longsword, longbow, 20 arrows.

Fey Lupes (12): HD 2; HP 15, 13x2, 12, 11, 10x3, 8, 7x2, 6; AC 7[12]; **Atk** 2 claws (1d4); **Move** 12 or pounce (30ft leap); **Save** 16; **AL** C; **CL/XP** 3/60; **Special:** darkvision (60ft), howl (1/day, each pack member gains 1 hp per fey lupe joining in), immune to charm and sleep, pounce (30ft leap), rend (if 2 claws hit target, additional 1d4 damage, save avoids). (see **Appendix A: New Monsters**)

10-1. Traveling in the Hartwood

While traveling in the Hartwood, it is an easy task to stay on the path that leads to the Eo Mughna. If the characters venture off the path, they have a 3-in-6 chance of an encounter for each hour of travel.

Hartwood Random Encounters

1d4	Encounter
1	6 fey lupes
2	1d4 swarms of insects
3	White stag
4	10 fey lupes

Fey Lupes (as needed): HD 2; AC 7[12]; **Atk** 2 claws (1d4); **Move** 12 or pounce (30ft leap); **Save** 16; **AL** C; **CL/XP** 3/60; **Special:** darkvision (60ft), howl (1/day, each pack member gains 1 hp per fey lupe joining in), immune to charm and sleep, pounce (30ft leap), rend (if 2 claws hit target, additional 1d4 damage, save avoids). (see **Appendix A: New Monsters**)

Swarms of Insects (1d4): HD 3; AC 7[12]; **Atk** swarm (1d6); **Move** 9 (fly); **Save** 14; **AL** N; **CL/XP** 4/120; **Special:** immune to blunt weapons.

White Stag: HD 2; AC 7[12]; **Atk** 2 antlers (1d6); **Move** 15; **Save** 16; **AL** N; **CL/XP** 2/30; **Special:** none.

10-2. Eo Mughna

At the center of the Hartwood stands Eo Mughna, the Mighty Yew, which is actually a magnificent oak tree with a bark that shimmers with a glint of silver and gold. Although it stands only about 50 feet tall, it dwarfs the smaller trees around it. The upper branches of the tree are laden with apples, hazelnuts, and acorns. The bark is flecked with tiny motes of silver and gold.

Seanche's Lament

The Seanche's goal is to finish the song he has been cursed to play, while Gnaddr's goal is to kill and sacrifice the willing Seanche in order to open the gates and release his army. The timeline of the Seanche allows for three potential outcomes in the Hartwood at the Eo Mughna:

1. The Characters Arrive First

If the characters arrive before the Seanche, they find **Gnaddr** waiting at the tree. He greets the characters cordially, as if they were expected. Hidden in the woods are **8 fey lupes**.

> "Ah. You've come to witness the arrival and to hear the dreadful singer's last lament? Find a spot to observe. Unless … oh yes, that's it, you've come to interfere."

At this exact moment, the fey lupes make a surprise attack on the characters, and the battle with Gnaddr begins in earnest.

2. The Characters Arrive with the Seanche

The characters arriving with the Seanche is the most disruptive outcome for Gnaddr's plans, and he immediately uses a *suggestion* spell to cause the Seanche to begin playing the cursed lute. Gnaddr's first attack on his first round is made with the silvered knife against the Eo Mughna. This causes the tree to bleed sap, and a glimmering thread forms between the Seanche and the Eo Mughna. This connection remains for as long as the Seanche continues to play. On the second round, the Seanche loses 1d6 hit points and a low mist rolls in from the forest. When the Seanche loses a total of 20 hit points, the **8 fey lupes** arrive out of the mist to aid Gnaddr if they have not already been killed. When the Seanche has no more hit points remaining, the misty bridge forms and Gnaddr's army is unstoppable.

3. The Seanche Arrives Before the Characters

If the Seanche arrives before the characters, Gnaddr's lieutenant and her troops escort him to the Eo Mughna if they are still able. Otherwise, the Seanche makes his way through the Hartwood, counting on the *transport via plants* effect of the cursed lute to keep him safe. When he arrives, Gnaddr is casually leaning against the Eo Mughna and idly toying with a silver dagger. Once the Seanche enters the clearing, the **8 fey lupes** slip through the trees in an ever-tightening circle. They remain outside the clearing until an unspoken signal from Gnaddr summons them to action. Gnaddr uses *suggestion* to have the Seanche play the cursed lute and begin opening the bridge of mists. For each day the characters are behind the Seanche's arrival, he loses 1d6 hit points. If he has already lost 20 hit points when the characters arrive, the **8 fey lupes** are baying at the Seanche's feet.

Gnaddr, Fey Lord Serpent Priest: HP 76; AC 2[17]; **Atk** *+1 flaming longsword* (1d8 + 1d6 fire) or +1 silver dagger (1d4+1) or slap (1d4); **Move** 12; **Save** 5; **AL** N; **CL/XP** 12/2000; **Special:** +1 or better magic weapons to hit, immune to charm and sleep, magic resistance (15%), spell-like abilities, spineless (−1 penalty to ranged attacks because of serpentine bobbing and weaving), stilling strike (3/day, target petrified for 1d4 rounds with successful slap, save resists), vulnerable to iron (200% damage).
  Spell-like abilities: at will—*charm person, faerie fire, light, sleep*; 3/day—*clairvoyance, dimension door, ESP, invisibility, mirror image, plant growth, polymorph self, suggestion*; 1/day—*ice storm*.
  Equipment: plate mail, *+1 flaming longsword, +1 silver dagger, arrow of direction, torc na goineog* (see **Appendix B: New Magic Items**).
Fey Lupes (8): HD 2; HP 13, 12, 10x2, 8, 5, 3x2; AC 7[12]; **Atk** 2 claws (1d4); **Move** 12 or pounce (30ft leap); **Save** 16; **AL** C; **CL/XP** 3/60; **Special:** darkvision (60ft), howl (1/day, each pack member gains 1 hp per fey lupe joining in), immune to charm and sleep, pounce (30ft leap), rend (if 2 claws hit target, additional 1d4 damage, save avoids). (see **Appendix A: New Monsters**)
The Seanche, Male Human Cursed Performer: HP 74; AC 7[12]; **Atk** *+1 longsword* (1d8+1); **Move** 12; **Save** 5; **AL** L; **CL/XP** 12/2000; **Special:** spells (cast as a 10th-level spellcaster).
Spells: 3/day—*charm person, cure light wounds, darkness 15ft radius, detect invisibility, invisibility, light, magic missile, obscuring mist, phantasmal force*; 2/day—*dispel magic, haste*; 1/day—*confusion, fear, hallucinatory terrain*; 1/week—*legend lore*.
Equipment: *+1 longsword*, leather armor, *uilleann pipes of reality* (see **Appendix B**).
Note: The Seanche is cursed by the uilleann pipes he carries. They force him to perform a song each night and are leading him toward the Hartwood.

Conclusion

If the ritual is stopped, the *uillean pipes of reality* shatter, lifting the Seanche's curse and causing Gnaddr, or his body, to be pulled into the mist by large dark shapes as snow begins to fall. After he is dragged into the mist, the *torc na goineog* (see **Appendix B: New Magic Items**) is tossed into the clearing and lands in front of the Eo Mughna.

The emerald naga queen arrives a short time later with all of her retinue; so many snakes arrive that they seem to carpet the forest. She thanks the characters for retrieving the *torc na goineog* for her. If the characters attempt to stop the emerald naga queen from taking the torc, she and her snakes attack. She has **6 emerald nagas, 10 juvenile emerald nagas,** and **10 swarms of poisonous snakes** with her. As the snakes make their way past the Eo Mughna and into the mist, a small wooden chest is left in front of the characters. The chest contains three golden statuettes of snakes with emerald eyes. Each statuette is wrapped in velvet. The statues are worth 740 gp each and measure about a foot tall. The people of this region tell the tale of the snakes leaving their land for many years to come, often conflating the story with the chaos the Seanche sowed and even acknowledging him as driving the snakes from the land.

SS'Thissk, Emerald Naga (Queen): HD 10; HP 76; AC 2[17]; **Atk** bite (1d8 + poison) and coils (2d6 + constrict); **Move** 15; **Save** 5; **AL** N; **CL/XP** 12/2000; **Special:** constrict (automatic 2d6 damage per round after successful coil attack), magic resistance (30%), phase strike (1/day, 50ft radius, 3d6 damage and knocked prone, save for half and avoid being knocked prone), poison (save or die), spells (as 10th-level caster). (see **Appendix A: New Monsters**)
  Spells: 1st—*faerie fire, magic missile*; 2nd—*heat metal, hold person, invisibility, obscuring mist*; 3rd—*fireball, remove curse*; 4th—*charm monster*; 5th—*raise dead*.
Emerald Nagas (Adults) (6): HD 8; HP 60, 56, 52, 48, 41, 39; AC 2[17]; **Atk** bite (1d8 + poison) and coils (2d6 + constrict); **Move** 15; **Save** 8; **AL** N; **CL/XP** 10/1400; **Special:** constrict (automatic 2d6 damage per round after successful coil attack), magic resistance (20%), poison (save or die), spells (as 8th-level caster). (see **Appendix A: New Monsters**)
  Spells: 1st—*faerie fire, magic missile*; 2nd—*heat metal, hold person, invisibility, obscuring mist*; 3rd—*fireball, remove curse*; 4th—*charm monster*; 5th—*raise dead*.
Emerald Nagas (Juveniles) (10): HD 5; HP 37, 33, 30, 29x2, 25, 22, 20, 18, 13; AC 5[14]; **Atk** bite (1d6 + poison) and coils (1d6 + constrict); **Move** 12; **Save** 12; **AL** N; **CL/XP** 5/240; **Special:** constrict (automatic 1d6 damage per round after successful coil attack), magic resistance (10%), poison (save or die). (see **Appendix A: New Monsters**)
Swarms of Poisonous Snakes (10): HD 2; HP 16, 14x2, 12, 10x3, 9, 6x2; AC 5[14]; **Atk** bite (1d6 + poison); **Move** 18; **Save** 18; **AL** N; **CL/XP** 2/30; **Special:** poison (+2 save or die).

Appendix A: New Monsters

The following NPCs and new monsters are found in *The Seanche's Lament*.

Bean Fionn

Hit Dice: 7
Armor Class: 7[12]
Attacks: claws (1d4)
Saving Throw: 9
Special: Beguiling kiss, drowning tide, immune to charm and sleep, resist cold
Move: 12/12 (swim)
Alignment: Neutrality
Number Encountered: 1d3
Challenge Level: 8/800

A bean fionn — also known as a drowning sidhe — is created when a fey creature fails in its vow to protect a body of water. The effects of this failure create a variety of drastic changes in a landscape: a lake goes dry, a small brook becomes a lake, a mountain spring becomes a raging waterfall, etc. The drowning sidhe, who is still bound to the area they failed to protect, transforms into a perversion of its former self, often re-enacting the very event that caused their failure. Although intelligent and still beautiful, they are volatile and unpredictable. A bean fionn attacks with her claws, but three times per day she can deliver a beguiling kiss. A target who fails a saving throw is charmed (as charm person) for one hour. The bean fionn can also cause a freezing wave of cold to radiate around her to do 2d6 points of damage to anyone within a 15-foot radius (save for half damage). Bean fionns are immune to charm and sleep spells, and take half damage from cold.

Bean Fionn: HD 7; AC 7[12]; **Atk** claws (1d4); **Move** 12 (swim 12); **Save** 9; **AL** N; **CL/XP** 8/800; **Special:** beguiling kiss (3/day, save or charmed for 1 hour), drowning tide (1/day, 15ft radius, 2d6 cold damage, save for half), immune to charm and sleep, resist cold (50% damage).

Each-Uisce

Hit Dice: 4
Armor Class: 7[12]
Attacks: kick (1d6)
Saving Throw: 13
Special: Resist cold, submerge
Move: 15 (swim)
Alignment: Neutrality
Number Encountered: 1d4+2
Challenge Level: 4/120

The each-uisce normally kicks to defend itself. It can also grab a target with a successful melee attack and quickly submerge, dragging the foe with it. The target must make a saving throw or be stunned for 1d3 rounds, taking 1 point of damage per round stunned.

Each-uisce: HD 4; AC 7[12]; **Atk** kick (1d6); **Move** 15 (swim); **Save** 13; **AL** N; **CL/XP** 4/120; **Special:** resist cold (50% damage), submerge (pull creature underwater with successful melee strike, save or stunned for 1d3 rounds, 1 point damage per round).

Ekimmu

Hit Dice: 8
Armor Class: 3[16]
Attacks: touch (3d4)
Saving Throw: 8
Special: malevolence, paralyzing howl, rejuvenate
Move: 0/12 (fly)
Alignment: Chaos
Number Encountered: 1d2
Challenge Level: 10/1,400

Ekimmu are the spirits of the dead who have not been given proper funerary rites. They may be murder victims cast into a defile, lonely hermits who died far away from others, or travelers too far from home for anyone to claim their corpses. Denied entry into the afterlife, they roam the world looking to vent their wrath upon mortals. They often do this by possessing a person and committing violent crimes, abandoning their victim when suspicions are aroused. Some legends say that an ekimmu can be quieted or even laid to rest if invited to a funerary feast and offered the appropriate libations.

Once per round an ekimmu can merge its body with a victim (as per the spell *magic jar*, except it doesn't require a receptacle). A failed saving throw allows the ekimmu to possess and control the victim. Three times per day, an ekimmu can unleash a fearsome howl that paralyzes everyone within 30 feet for 1d4 + 1 rounds (save avoids). An ekimmu is difficult to destroy and rejuvenates in 2d6 days; the only way to permanently destroy one is to determine the reason for its existence and set right whatever prevents it from entering the underworld. Animals do not willingly approach within 30 feet of an ekimmu.

Ekimmu: HD 8; AC 3[16]; **Atk** touch (3d4); **Move** 0 (fly 12); **Save** 8; **AL** N; **CL/XP** 10/1400; **Special:** malevolence (1/round, can possess and control target, as *magic jar*, save avoids), paralyzing howl (3/day, 30ft radius, save or paralyzed for 1d4+1 rounds), rejuvenate (returns in 2d6 days).

	Air	Earth/Stone	Fire	Water
Hit Dice:	7	9	10	8
Armor Class:	1[18]	3[16]	3[16]	4[15]
Attacks:	bite (1d6), tail smash (2d4)	bite (1d6), tail smash (2d4)	bite (1d6), tail smash (2d4)	bite (1d6), tail smash (2d4)
Saving Throw:	9	6	5	8
Special:	whirlwind	avalanche, immune to slashing and piercing weapons	fire breath, immune to fire, vulnerable to cold	drown, vulnerable to fire
Move:	15	15	15	15
Alignment:	Neutrality	Neutrality	Neutrality	Neutrality
Number Encountered:	1d3	1d2	1d2	1d3
Challenge Level:	8/800	10/1,400	11/1,700	9/1,100

An elemental adder is a snake made up of the elements of its home plane. These creatures are much more intelligent than many are wont to believe, and rumors even exist of ancient and powerful elemental adders who have mastered the arcane arts.

All elemental adders have special attacks related to their home planes:
- Three times per day, the air adder can bite its tail and spin in a circle to create a tornado that tosses foes 1d3 x 10 feet. Creatures take 1d6 points of damage per 10 feet they are thrown.
- The fire adder deals an additional 1d6 points of fire damage with its bite and tail smash. Three times per day, it can breathe a cone of fire up to 15 feet that does 3d6 points of damage (save for half).
- The earth adder is immune to slashing and piercing weapons. Three times per day, it can cause a 30-foot line of rocks to slam into any target in the path of destruction. All targets take 3d6 points of damage (save for half).
- The water adder's bite injects water into the target and causes it to drown if it fails a saving throw. A drowning creature takes an additional 1d6 points of damage.

Elemental Adder (Air): HD 7; AC 1[18]; **Atk** bite (1d6), tail smash (2d4); **Move** 15; **Save** 9; **AL** N; **CL/XP** 8/800; **Special:** whirlwind (3/day, spin in a tornado-like twirl, save or tossed 1d3x10 feet, 1d6 damage per 10ft thrown).

Elemental Adder (Earth/Stone): HD 9; AC 3[16]; **Atk** bite (1d6), tail smash (2d4); **Move** 15; **Save** 6; **AL** N; **CL/XP** 10/1400; **Special:** avalanche (3/day, 30ft line, 3d6 damage, save for half), immune to slashing and piercing weapons.

Elemental Adder (Fire): HD 10; AC 3[16]; **Atk** bite (1d6 + 1d6 fire), tail smash (2d4 + 1d6 fire); **Move** 15; **Save** 5; **AL** N; **CL/XP** 11/1700; **Special:** fire breath (3/day, 3d6 damage, save for half), immune to fire, vulnerable to cold (200% damage).

Elemental Adder (Water): HD 8; AC 4[15]; **Atk** bite (1d6 + bloat), tail smash (2d4); **Move** 15; **Save** 8; **AL** N; **CL/XP** 9/1100; **Special:** drown (1d6 damage, save avoids), vulnerable to fire (200% damage).

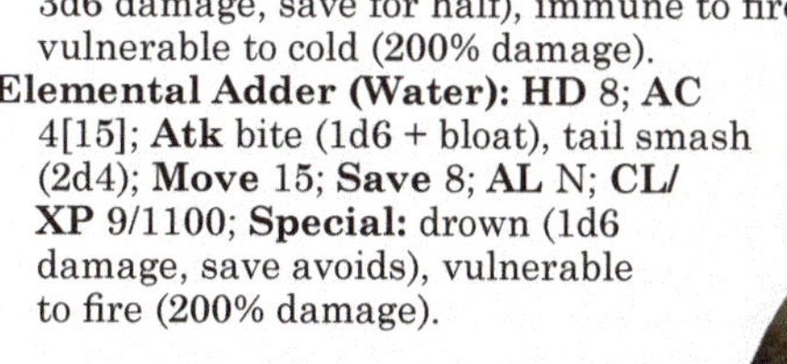

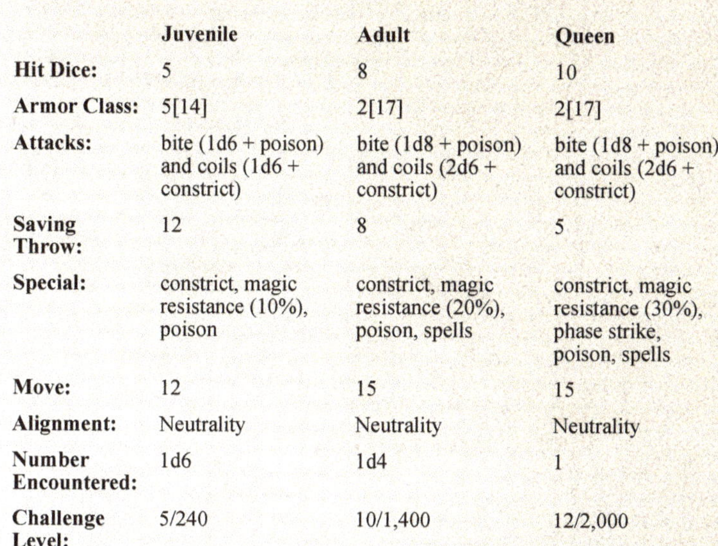

	Juvenile	Adult	Queen
Hit Dice:	5	8	10
Armor Class:	5[14]	2[17]	2[17]
Attacks:	bite (1d6 + poison) and coils (1d6 + constrict)	bite (1d8 + poison) and coils (2d6 + constrict)	bite (1d8 + poison) and coils (2d6 + constrict)
Saving Throw:	12	8	5
Special:	constrict, magic resistance (10%), poison	constrict, magic resistance (20%), poison, spells	constrict, magic resistance (30%), phase strike, poison, spells
Move:	12	15	15
Alignment:	Neutrality	Neutrality	Neutrality
Number Encountered:	1d6	1d4	1
Challenge Level:	5/240	10/1,400	12/2,000

An emerald naga is a long snake with glittering viridian scales that appear to be dusted with crushed gems. A large yet exquisite feminine human face tops the thickly muscled snake body. Fangs clearly protrude from the creature's mouth. These creatures can be friendly if approached cautiously. They are intelligent and curious.

The emerald naga attacks with a poisonous bite and by wrapping a creature in its coils. A creature hit by the coils takes automatic constriction damage each round until freed.

The natural jewel-encrusted scales of the emerald naga grant it magic resistance depending on its age.

A juvenile emerald naga is a seven-foot-long snake with glittering viridian scales that appear to be dusted with crushed gems. Its face appears to be that of an adolescent human female.

An adult emerald naga is between 20 and 30 feet long, with an adult woman's face. They are competent and dangerous spellcasters.

The emerald naga queen's head is larger than that of a humanoid and is proportional to her 30-foot-long body. The larger naga is a dangerous spellcaster who uses a mix of spells. Once per day, the emerald naga queen can unleash a phase strike of energy that strikes all creatures within a 50-foot radius. Anyone caught in the wave of force takes 3d6 points of damage and is knocked prone unless they make a saving throw for half damage and to avoid being knocked down.

Emerald Naga (Juvenile): HD 5; AC 5[14]; **Atk** bite (1d6 + poison) and coils (1d6 + constrict); **Move** 12; **Save** 12; **AL** N; **CL/XP** 5/240; **Special:** constrict (automatic 1d6 damage per round after successful coil attack), magic resistance (10%), poison (save or die).

Emerald Naga (Adult): HD 8; AC 2[17]; **Atk** bite (1d8 + poison) and coils (2d6 + constrict); **Move** 15; **Save** 8; **AL** N; **CL/XP** 10/1400; **Special:** constrict (automatic 2d6 damage per round after successful coil attack), magic resistance (20%), poison (save or die), spells (as 8th-level caster).

Spells: 1st—*faerie fire, magic missile*; 2nd—*heat metal, hold person, invisibility, obscuring mist*; 3rd—*fireball, remove curse*; 4th—*charm monster*; 5th—*raise dead*.

Emerald Naga (Queen): HD 10; AC 2[17]; **Atk** bite (1d8 + poison) and coils (2d6 + constrict); **Move** 15; **Save** 5; **AL** N; **CL/XP** 12/2000; **Special:** constrict (automatic 2d6 damage per round after successful coil attack), magic resistance (30%), phase strike (1/day, 50ft radius, 3d6 damage and knocked prone, save for half and avoid being knocked prone), poison (save or die), spells (as 10th-level caster).

Spells: 1st—*faerie fire, magic missile*; 2nd—*heat metal, hold person, invisibility, obscuring mist*; 3rd—*fireball, remove curse*; 4th—*charm monster*; 5th—*raise dead*.

Fear Ghorta

Hit Dice: 8
Armor Class: 6[13]
Attacks: withering touch (1d6)
Saving Throw: 8
Special: Famish, howl, hungry grass, vulnerable to fire
Move: 12
Alignment: Chaos
Number Encountered: 1d3
Challenge Level: 10/1,400

The fear ghorta is the emaciated figure of a starved person who still lies in an unshriven grave. It is possible to find the graves because of the patches of what are known as "hungry grass" that grow over their buried corpses and drain life from any living creature within reach. The spirit itself is a manifestation from the corpse and melts away if destroyed, only to return the next night.

A fear ghorta attacks with a withering touch. Three times per day, it can unleash a famishing aura in a 30-foot radius. Any creature caught in this aura must make a saving throw or take 1d6 points of damage for 1d4 rounds. During this time, they are compelled to consume any available food. Each night, a fear ghorta can unleash a terrifying howl of pain that causes any creatures that hear the sound to be unable to sleep. Creatures suffer a −1 penalty to hit, damage, and saves for the next day.

epatch of covering a fear ghorta's grave   creatures within a 60-foot radius of the patch of grass take 1d6 points of damage per hour (no save) as the grass drains their lifeforce. it

Fear ghortas take double damage from fire.

Fear Ghorta: HD 8; AC 6[13]; **Atk** withering touch (1d6); **Move** 12; **Save** 8; **AL** C; **CL/XP** 10/1400; **Special:** famish (3/day, 30ft radius, save or take 1d6 damage for 1d4 rounds and eat any available food), hungry grass (60ft radius, drain life, 1d6 damage per hour), howl (save or unable to sleep, −1 penalty to hit, damage, and saves until able to rest), vulnerable to fire (200% damage).

Fey Lord

Hit Dice: 7
Armor Class: 2[17]
Attacks: rapier (1d6) or slap (1d4)
Saving Throw: 9
Special: +1 or better magic weapons to hit, immune to charm and sleep, magic resistance (15%), spell-like abilities, vulnerable to iron
Move: 12
Alignment: Neutrality
Number Encountered: 1
Challenge Level: 8/800

This refined young lord exudes an aura of command and grace, and those around him seem compelled to obey. He looks down upon those around him with a haughty look of derision that makes it clear you are less than he. He wears a set of field plate that is nearly formfitting and seems to hug his body. The glint of golden mail sparkles between the armored plates.

The fey lord can be hit only by magic weapons. Spells have a 15% chance of not affecting the creature. The fey lord is vulnerable to iron weapons and takes double damage from successful strikes with such weapons.

Fey Lord: HD 7; AC 2[17]; **Atk** rapier (1d6) or slap (1d4); **Move** 12; **Save** 9; **AL** N; **CL/XP** 8/800; **Special:** +1 or better magic weapons to hit, immune to charm and sleep, magic resistance (15%), spell-like abilities, vulnerable to iron (200% damage).

Spell-like abilities: at will—*charm person, faerie fire, light, sleep;* 3/day—*clairvoyance, dimension door, ESP, invisibility, plant growth, polymorph self;* 1/day—*ice storm.*

Fey Lupe

Hit Dice: 2
Armor Class: 7[12]
Attacks: 2 claws (1d4)
Saving Throw: 16
Special: darkvision (60ft), howl, immune to charm and sleep, pounce, rend
Move: 12
Alignment: Chaos
Number Encountered: 1d4, 2d4
Challenge Level: 3/60

The dark eyes of these long-limbed wolf-like creatures betray their intelligence. They hunt in packs, using stealth and teamwork to dispatch a foe. They often serve as bodyguards and soldiers for stronger fey creatures. Their thick fur is often painted with dark red symbols and runes, some still dripping in the blood of their victims. If a fey lupe strikes a target with both claw attacks, it deals an additional 1d4 points of damage if the target fails a saving throw. A fey lupe can leap up to 30 feet. Once per day, a fey lupe can begin howling to regain 1 point of damage. If the pack is together, other fey lupes begin howling as well, and all members heal a number of points equal to the total number of creatures (so 6 points healed if six fey lupe join in). Fey lupe are immune to sleep and charm spells.

Fey Lupe: HD 2; AC 7[12]; **Atk** 2 claws (1d4); **Move** 12 or pounce (30ft leap); **Save** 16; **AL** C; **CL/XP** 3/60; **Special:** darkvision (60ft), howl (1/day, each pack member gains 1 hp per fey lupe joining in), immune to charm and sleep, pounce (30ft leap), rend (if 2 claws hit target, additional 1d4 damage, save avoids).

Filth Fairy

Hit Dice: 4
Armor Class: 5[14]
Attacks: 2 claws (1d4)
Saving Throw: 13
Special: Slime breath, spell-like abilities
Move: 12/12/12 (fly, swim)
Alignment: Chaos
Number Encountered: 1d6, 2d8
Challenge Level: 5/240

These small fey creatures superficially look like sprites, save for the ooze and filth that covers their body and the slightly ravenous look on their small faces. Acid sizzles as it drips from their tiny pointed teeth and sharp claws.

These small fey are often at home in the deepest, darkest swamps, where they revel in the muck and filth of the marsh. They delight in the pollution of clean waters and actively try to expand their contaminated realms. These fey also ally themselves with creatures who enjoy the same environments and even sometimes cultivate swamp oozes and other denizens of the bog. Filth fairies are sometimes found serving a green hag, or, rarely, a coven of green hags, with whom they work to control their swampy paradise.

Filth Fairy: HD 4; AC 5[14]; Atk 2 claws (1d4 + 1d3 acid); **Move** 12 (fly 12, swim 12); **Save** 13; **AL** C; **CL/XP** 5/240; **Special:** acidic (additional 1d3 damage), slime breath (3/day, 15ft cone, 3d6 acid damage, save for half), spell-like abilities.

Spell-like abilities: at will—*faerie fire, obscuring mist*; 3/day— *phantasmal force*.

Giant Pike

Hit Dice: 11
Armor Class: 3[16]
Attacks: bite (3d6), tail slap (2d6)
Saving Throw: 4
Special: Swallow
Move: 18 (swim) or 30-foot leap
Alignment: Neutrality
Number Encountered: 1d3
Challenge Level: 11/1700

This 20-foot length of muscle and scale is an apex river predator that has grown too large for the shallow currents from which it spawned. The giant pike can leap out of the water and cover up to 30 feet. If the giant pike rolls a natural 20 to hit with its bite attack, it swallows the target whole. A swallowed creature takes 2d6 points of damage per round.

Giant Pike: HD 11; AC 3[16]; Atk bite (3d6), tail slap (2d6); **Move** 18 (swim) or 30ft leap; **Save** 4; **AL** N; **CL/XP** 11/1700; **Special:** swallow (natural 20 to hit, 2d6 damage per round).

Phooka

Hit Dice: 4
Armor Class: 5[14]
Attacks: weapon (1d3)
Saving Throw: 13
Special: Alternate form, spell-like abilities, spell resistance (16%), tree stride
Move: 6
Alignment: Neutrality
Number Encountered: 1d3, 2d4
Challenge Level: 5/240

Phookas are tricksters and jokesters. They revel in playing tricks on unwary travelers, leading them on merry chases or getting them lost deep in the forest. They are not necessarily malicious though some phookas do lean toward evil and murder.

A phooka's trickery may include turning itself into an enchanted pony and offer a stranger a ride, only to lead it through brambles and thorns at top speed, or to lead travelers to enchanted springs that cause them to fall into a deep slumber and strip them of all their belongings and clothes, then leave behind clues as to where their possessions are hidden.

Phookas are deeply attuned to nature and animals and have a bond with their natural surroundings. If slain, all plant matter within one square mile of the phooka withers and dies.

A phooka stands about three feet tall.

Phooka: HD 4; AC 5[14]; Atk weapon (1d3); **Move** 6; **Save** 13; **AL** N; **CL/XP** 5/240; **Special:** alternate form (at will, mountain lion or wolf), dancing lights (3/day, moving balls of light), spell resistance (16%), tree stride (enter tree and move up to 50ft to another tree).

Summer Knight

Hit Dice: 10
Armor Class: 3[16]
Attacks: weapon (1d8)
Saving Throw: 5
Special: Magic resistance (10%), nature's grace, vulnerable to iron
Move: 12
Alignment: Lawful
Number Encountered: 1d3, 2d4
Challenge Level: 12/2,000

The summer knight is a fey creature bound to the summer court. Its voice is like honey, its smile a beam of light. Grace and the swiftness and ferocity of a jungle cat are wrapped in the charming and warm exterior of the handsome elfin humanoid. It controls the natural magic of the world around it with ease.

Three times per day,

Summer Knight: HD 10; AC 3[16]; Atk weapon (1d8); **Move** 12; **Save** 5; **AL** L; **CL/XP** 12/2000; **Special:** magic resistance (10%), nature's grace (3/day, 60ft radius, cause green tendril to bloom healing pollen, heal 3d6 damage), vulnerable to iron (200% damage).

Swarm of Grigs

Hit Dice: 7
Armor Class: 6[13]
Attacks: Swarm (2d6)
Saving Throw: 9
Special: Fiddle, spell-like abilities
Move: 6/9 (fly)
Alignment: Neutrality
Number Encountered: 1d4
Challenge Level: 8/800

A grig swarm is a large mass of flying grigs. The individual grigs that make up the swarm have light blue skin, forest-green hair, and brown hairy legs, and usually wear tunics or brightly colored vests with buttons made from tiny gems. A grig stands 1-1/2 feet tall and weighs about one pound. They attack with weapons, or use their fiddles to cause a victim to dance uncontrollably (save avoids). Once per day, a grig can cast *polymorph self*, *plant growth*, *invisibility* and *pyrotechnics*.

Swarm of Grigs: HD 7; AC 6[13]; Atk swarm (2d6); **Move** 6 (fly 9); **Save** 9; **AL** N; **CL/XP** 8/800; **Special:** fiddle, spell-like abilities.

Appendix B: New Magic Items

New magic items found in this adventure are described in this appendix.

Brighid's Raiment and Arms

Brighid's Raiment and Arms are a breastplate, shield, and spear.

Brighid's Breastplate

This bronze breastplate is etched in flame-like patterns of rams facing one another, heads lowered to charge. The breastplate is remarkably light and if you are of good alignment, it emits a soft golden glow. While you wear this armor, you gain a +1 bonus to your armor class and you are immune to being charmed and take half damage from fire.

Brighid's Spear

The spearhead is about 20 inches long and has a "flame blade" of shallow waves. It shows signs of use in the many nicks and scratches in the metal. It attaches to a six-and-a-half-foot hardwood pole to create a *+1 spear*. After you hit a creature with the spear, once per day you may cause an additional 4d6 points of fire damage to that creature. The spear cannot be used in this way again until the following morning at dawn.

Brighid's Shield

Brighid's shield gleams when lifted and is difficult to look at for long because of the reflected light. While using this shield, you gain a +1 bonus to your armor class. Once per day, you may use the shield to cast *light*.

Miscellaneous Magical Item, Greater

Torc na Goineog

The torc of the serpents is said to signify its wearer as the king of serpents and grants commensurate power. While wearing the torc, you gain a +2 bonus to saving throws and are immune to poison. You can speak with and understand any serpents. You may cast *snake charm* at will. You can also transform into any serpent type creature of 10 hit dice or less once per week. This transformation lasts until you are knocked unconscious or resume your original form. You always assume your original form at full hit points. You may cast *monster summoning V* but may summon only serpents and snakes as detailed in the table below:

Serpent Monster Summoning

1d6	Monster Summoned
1	Giant viper
2	Giant constrictor
3	Giant spitting snake
4	Amphisbaena
5	1d4 + 6 swarms of poisonous snakes
6	Adult emerald naga

Amphisbaena: HD 5; AC 5[14]; Atk 2 bite (1d3 + poison); **Move** 10; **Save** 12; **AL** N; **CL/XP** 7/600; **Special:** lethal poison (save or die). (*Monstrosities* 440)

Giant Viper (or Cobra): HD 4; AC 5[14]; Atk bite (1d3 + poison); **Move** 12; **Save** 13; **AL** N; **CL/XP** 6/400; **Special:** lethal poison (save or die). (*Monstrosities* 440)

Giant Constrictor: HD 6; AC 5[14]; Atk bite (1d3), constrict (2d4); **Move** 10; **Save** 11; **AL** N; **CL/XP** 7/600; **Special:** constrict (automatic 2d4 damage after hit; 1-in-6 chance to pin limb). (*Monstrosities* 440)

Giant Spitting Snake: HD 4; AC 5[14]; Atk bite (1d3 + poison) or spit poison; **Move** 13; **Save** 11; **AL** N; **CL/XP** 6/400; **Special:** spit or bite with lethal poison (40ft range). (*Monstrosities* 440)

Emerald Naga (Adult): HD 8; AC 2[17]; Atk bite (1d8 + poison) and coils (2d6 + constrict); **Move** 15; **Save** 8; **AL** N; **CL/XP** 10/1400; **Special:** constrict (automatic 2d6 damage per round after successful coil attack), magic resistance (20%), poison (save or die), spells (as 8th-level caster). (see **Appendix A: New Monsters**)
Spells: 1st—*faerie fire, magic missile;* 2nd—*heat metal, hold person, invisibility, obscuring mist;* 3rd—*fireball, remove curse;* 4th—*charm monster;* 5th—*raise dead.*

Swarms of Poisonous Snakes (1d4+6): HD 2; AC 5[14]; Atk bite (1d6 + poison); **Move** 18; **Save** 18; **AL** N; **CL/XP** 2/30; **Special:** poison (+2 save or die).

Miscellaneous Magical Items, Medium

Leprechaun's Gold

Leprechaun's gold consists of a group of saucer-sized gold coins with a great glyph on one face and a snake eating its tail on the opposite face. If a creature other than the leprechaun who owns the coins opens their container, the coins immediately burst into a cloud of tiny golden-winged snakes. The snakes disperse and attempt to hide. A character may attempt to spot the *leprechaun's gold* by rolling 3d6 vs. 3d6 rolled by the coins. The higher number wins. If the coins win, the character doesn't find any coins. If the character wins, he or she spots a number of coins equal to the difference between the two rolls (so if the character rolls an 18 and the coins roll a 7, then 11 coins are found). Once spotted, *leprechaun's gold* may be acquired. Once captured, a flying snake reverts to a coin. *Leprechaun's gold* is worth 10 gp per coin. They are usually found in caches of 1d100 + 8 coins. If they are gathered in a group of nine or more coins, they attempt to escape and hide again. They always try to escape to their original owner.

Weapons

Deadly Whisper

This elegantly crafted +1 blade slices the air with barely a whisper, and the pommel is adorned with a gleaming black opal that seems to drink the light around it. Three times per day, you may create silence in a 10-foot radius. To end the silence, the blade must be sheathed; otherwise, the silence remains for 1d6 + 4 minutes. The first time the silence is used against a target, the wielder gains a +1 bonus to hit.

Feyslayer Sword

This heavy +1 blade is crafted from meteoric iron and always feels cold to the touch. Once per day, you may grant an ally of your choice within 30 feet of you a +1 bonus on an attack roll or saving throw. If you have fey ancestry or are an elf, you have a −1 penalty on all attack rolls made with the blade.

Cursed Item

Luricawne Shoes

These exquisitely crafted shoes conform to the feet of any creature who wears them. When you put the shoes on, you must make a saving throw or immediately begin dancing. You may continue to move as long as it involves dancing. The character takes 1d6 points of damage per hour from the pain. *Remove curse* allows the wearer to remove the shoes.

Uillean Pipes of Reality

Uillean pipes of reality cause a single song of its choice to manifest into reality once per day. The magic of the pipes approximates the song with as close a proxy as it can identify. The uillean pipes compel you to travel, and you may not stay in the same town, village, or camp twice. You must perform before a crowd at least once per day, and you must perform a song of the pipes' choosing during that performance. You may use the pipes to cast the following spells without material components:

At will: *transport via plants*
3/day: *dimension door*

In combat, the pipes can work to protect their wielder. If cornered, the pipes emit a heavy, dull note. All creatures within 60 feet other than the wielder who hear the note must make a saving throw with a −4 penalty or be petrified for 12 hours.

www.ingramcontent.com/pod-product-compliance
Lightning Source LLC
Chambersburg PA
CBHW041202100726
47911CB00016B/836